# View from the Tent

**Atreus**

Seattle, Washington, USA

ISBN #: 978-1-4357-1339-0

Printed in the United States of America.

*In Neglect*

*They leave us so to the way we took,*
*As two in whom them were proved*
*mistaken,*
*That we sit sometimes in the wayside*
*nook,*
*With mischievous, vagrant, seraphic*
*look,*
*And try if we cannot feel forsaken.*

*Robert Frost*

# PREFACE

Thoughts, letters and notes from Atreus were shared with me over a number of years. He was a homeless man living primarily in an outdoor shelter in Seattle.

These musings come from a man who was crushed by violence and loss. His reflections give hope to many who find themselves in similar situations living on the outskirts of society.

Usually, I would be handed a hand written sheet folded up into a small square. These were given as surreptitiously as possible with little fanfare being paid to how they were passed to me.

Over time I would ask questions or hand him a question I had written out for his consideration. Sometimes I would get an answer and other times I would be ignored.

Many of his notes were posted on our Let Kids Be Kids website or shared with groups in order to humanize those we often ignore. His stories of fellow homeless seem to touch a cord with people much more than statistics and bland descriptions of the poor and homeless.

I have not included all of his notes. Only those that seem to be related to his journey are in this small book.

I was one of a number of volunteers that interacted with various homeless people in shelters, on the streets and in the city. I am not sure why he chose me, but I am proud and touched by his trust and openness.

His thoughts and observations dovetail with my experiences and insights into a group of people that are often marginalized for their station in society.

I have tried to transcribe accurately his very challenging handwriting. On occasion I have added a word or two if I could not make out the script. I hope I have made the right choices when I made these changes.

I regret that I never considered he would leave Seattle before I had an opportunity to go over his writings with him with publishing in mind.

If he ever sees this little book I hope it brings a smile to his face.

In respect to all those in similar circumstances net proceeds will be donated to those serving the poor, the sick and the homeless.

M. Barrett Miller

2008

2

# 1

Thank God we are moving out of Tukwila!  The last months have been a challenge with torrential rains, freezes, and the occasional rat seeking warmth in my tent, or, worse yet, my sleeping bag.

Tomorrow we move to Saint Mark's Cathedral on Capital Hill. Because of various regulations our population shrunk to twenty-six shivering residents in Tukwila. The move will allow us to grow back to our usual population of around a hundred needy souls.

Moving to the Cathedral will be like staying at the Pierre, the Plaza, the Mark Hopkins, or, many other five star hotels I frequented before life delivered me to the comforts of sleeping on a shipping pallet.

My story is not unique so I won't dwell on the circumstances that brought me to this place in my life.

What I want to share is the loneliness and sense of being disconnected from meaningful rapport with anyone.

"The biggest disease today is the feeling of being unwanted. People need to be loved, without love, people die." Princess Diana, Kosovo

I saw that quote in a discarded Time Magazine. It seemed directed at us rather than the people of Kosovo she was speaking to at the time.

Everything that was is no more. Human touch, flirting, conversation, desire conveyed through a look, hugging, and yes, being held closely for a kiss saying I love and need you. All gone.

There was a time when I could have thought my way out of this dilemma that faces me every day. Where did I lose the ability to survive?

Perhaps Swift's "A Modest Proposal" should be dusted off and used as a primer for dealing with us.

2

Before moving into the site on Cherry Hill the local community wanted to meet us before giving approval of the move.

It is understandable that any community would not want to interact with this band of rovers, but it is also hard on our collective egos to be viewed as less than desirable.

I'd been to two previous community meetings and had a good idea of the preconceptions, prejudices and fear aimed at us as we move into a neighborhood.I tried to share this with some of my fellow campers but most of them were naïve to what objections might be raised by good people motivated by a number of fears, both internal and external.

Are we all alcoholics, drug addicts, mentally afflicted, potential child molesters, thieves, bums, lazy, carbuncles on society etc?

I've heard all of these, and worse!

Fortunately there are some great people supporting us that speak up when these questions are posed.

I never say anything and attempt to shrink from the light when possible.

I sometimes think our supporters have it almost as challenging as do we. I mean, does anyone really respect people that do so much for free? Ah, they must be church people that are suppose to be doing this God's work!

I wonder how many of you are closer than you think to be becoming my tent mate!

Well, we survived our interview and will move into a nice site in an established neighborhood.

I once visited the city dump in Brasilia to be told more than a hundred thousand children lived there from birth to death.

I lay my head down on my jacket and thank my lucky stars I'm not a kid.    Atreus

3

The other day a group of High School kids dropped by to deliver lunches and take a tour of our "city."

I stepped away from the greeters, as I didn't want to be in a position to be asked to lead the tour or share "my story" with any of them.

One of the younger guys stepped up and led them around the camp pointing out one or another thing of interest. Really, are rows of tents, a TV tent and a makeshift kitchen of interest? What they really wanted to know was what in hell were people doing hunkered down in tents in America!! Who and why are we?

When the group gathered around our community table to talk with a number of the residents I gave the slightest of signals to one of our patrons that I wanted no part of this particular interaction. He seems to be fairly intuitive as he picked up on my signal allowing me to stay seated rather than the obvious physical dodge and flight.

The young tour leader graduated from High School four years ago and told the kids it was methamphetamines that knocked him out of culinary school. I could see their eyes were beginning to open to the possibilities that they could be closer to our reality than they thought a few minutes ago.

A number of people sitting around the table began to open up to these kids. I felt a cold horror beginning to work it's way up my legs …

James, one of the campers, had been a shrimp fisherman down in the Gulf. He was totally wiped out by hurricane Katrina. About 2000 were relocated to Seattle from the New Orleans area within weeks of the storm. He lost everything including his two dogs. His upside is the huge check that is in the process of liberating him from our camp. He said he was heading up to Alaska. Good luck, James.

Claire, poor soul, has been lost in the Coney Island of her mind for years. Ferlinghetti wrote a great poem with that image in the title. Oh, well! A combination of abuse, few skills combined with booze and drugs has wizened her mind beyond repair. She is cheerful and told the kids to stay in school and love God. Couldn't have said it better myself if I had the ability to say anything.

Marvin, another camper, is a strange duck indeed. He speaks like a solicitor trying to outwit Rumpole. Hard to know if he's just off, or, a genius taking a sabbatical. He told the kids some whopper about avoiding debt collectors who were unrelenting in their pursuit. I guess he is nuts! Good for him.

Not many people left at the table to shelter me. Time to go kiddies!

8

Fortunately, their person returned with the bus signaling them the visit was over.

Goodbyes, good lucks and see ya next summer were exchanged by all. Nice kids.

I don't know what I think and feel? Am I jealous of their youth and potential or secure in my path with all its meanderings? Too many mysteries.

4

You haven't heard from me lately as I was cooped up in a state facility in northern California. The weather was great but hanging out with mentally challenged inmates was not what I had in mind when I headed into the wine country.

Maybe I'll share some of that story later.

What spurred me to write again was the visit of high school kids to our shelter last week. As in the past, I stayed on the periphery avoiding talking with any of these kids as they wondered what we were doing living in tents surrounded by million dollar houses. Hell, I wonder the same all the time...

Anyway, one kid diplomatically challenged one of our long term residents on why he was still here years later with some wildly transparent tale of the government inhibiting his opportunities. A one legged armadillo could see through that defense. The kid didn't miss a beat and asked why the guy didn't get a job at McDonald's, or anywhere, other than living in a tent. Our guy dodged and weaved but was carried out of the ring by head shaking attendants.

So, what's the point?

The guy is scared to death to take a risk. Who knows what happened to make life better in a tent city than out in the crowd throwing punches to consume and survive. I better slow down!

Fear...do I know it wherever it hides.

This isn't working too well.

Atreus

# 5

Thanks for helping out and arranging the volunteers.

Someone told me they came from Starbucks. That's nice.

Lets see, I've made these moves about eight times and each time I am surprised that it all works without a major incident. No fist fights or murders though throwing a well-aimed punch has crossed my mind numerous times. A little bit of power in the wrong hands can make it unpleasant for all of us. The "move master" did a good job in his gentle way.

Our new site is a challenge due to the closeness of each other to each other. Most know to leave me alone which is just fine. I am so used to being alone I hardly allow the thoughts of camaraderie or intimacy to walk around in my mind.

One of the women who was volunteering reminded me of someone who lives warmly a long time ago. My image of her is fuzzy. Maybe the lack of clarity is created by how I would breathe in every view of her knowing she was just passing through...desperate to chisel everything about her into the deepest corridors of my mind so I could conjure her at will. She has become like smoke. Here and gone in the same instant. What I wouldn't do to relive but one of those many glances we shared.

I came close to thinking about saying something to the memory jarring volunteer, but couldn't think of what to say with any semblance of maintaining any dignity I might have left. I don't look as I once did and I probably carry a faint odor of yesterday's meals and urine on my clothes.

The doorway out seems slammed closed.

Thanks for not bothering me further than taking these scribblings. I don't know if you respect me or not, but, I like your style and walk.

6

Thanks for the note of thanks. I'm ok with you doing whatever you like with these musings as long as I don't play a role in any of your schemes.

Maybe we could share coffee though don't start making plans or writing it down in that calendar you always seem to have in hand.

I noticed the other day that you picked up on the fact that there has been a little girl living here in camp. She's around eleven and sharing a tent with her mom. I have mixed feelings on her being here as this isn't a place I'd want one of my kids under any circumstances. The problem is that there are few shelters in the area that will accept a mother and child. There are none that will allow a man to be with a child. No wonder drugs and alcohol play the role they do here. Yes, that's the smell of crack! Truth is that it is safer here than on the streets. Can you believe it!!!

Kid is gone. Big camp meeting, lots of shouting, finger pointing and other craziness with the result being that she jeopardized the legitimacy of the camp by being here. I don't know where she went but can only hope it was a step up from here.

Everyone agreed to behave around the girl but this can't be the solution that the greater, more affluent, population wants for it's marginalized neighbors. Invisibility.

I know I come back to this theme but it feels as if we would be ok if we were just a little more invisible. Behind a bigger fence, wall, hedge so the innocent couldn't see us.

A couple of the college students you had here seemed truly interested, emphatic and empathetic on our challenge.

I so wanted to say something when our resident blowhard was showing off for the two young ladies. He was creating illusion from no cloth at all.

For whatever reasons the one blonde girl kept gazing in my direction. All I could think of was that even glass casts a reflection. I truly don't seem to exist at times casting no humanity or presence.

I need a break from all this...

Atreus

# 7

It was inevitable!

In our micro village of hope, despair, diversity, loneliness, new found friendships, charity and community, roamed death.

She arrived sometime during the night of the 21st to invite Michael Robinson to take the trip of a "life time" exiting our camp gently in to the hands of strangers.

It was comforting to see the respect, concern, and yes, some grief, on the faces of our fellow campers as Michael made his exit.

Do we need any stronger reminders to the sounds of times winged chariot hurrying near. Near to all of us living here. We are all probably wondering just what the hell has led us down the road to residing in a tent shelter with people one would generally avoid. I never would have spoken to the majority of people I don't speak to today.

Death reminds and equalizes all of us. The ultimate democratization!

The local preacher did a nice job putting together a small candle-light service. Some of the people who continually support us brought flowers and some munchies. It was a nice thing for them to do...

Some of our fellow campers said some kind words about Michael. I hope his family is having similar thoughts. I wonder if they know he has died?

I didn't know you and I'm saddened I didn't know your name was Michael. In the likeness of God, if I remember accurately.

Had I been able to say something I would have said I was sorry I didn't care more and to wish you a safe voyage.

Atreus

8

Thank you for all the cd's you left here the other day. Fortunately, I saw you drop them off giving me the opportunity to go through the stack before anyone else got a shot. What a joy to find The Three Tenors and Pavarotti's last compilation. I haven't felt a wave of happiness like that in ages!!

One of my many life's great memories is seeing Pavarotti perform in the Wiener Staatsoper.

I stayed in the Hotel Sacher which is mere light years from this place. We shared horse drawn carriage rides to the park to listen to Mozart. Bread, wine, cheese and incredible music in one of the great parks of Europe.

You've got to imagine that when Pavarotti gets to heaven he will be asked to step in the garden and give the Lord a song or two...

Sometimes I wonder if this is really me.

There has been a lot of tension here lately as we approach yet another move. The rumor is that we are going south of Seattle.

Anywhere is good but distance creates lots of problems for many who call this place home. You know, doctor's appointments and the like.

Perhaps you and your want to do good folk should attempt to put together a predictable schedule for this wandering camp. Consistency might reinforce a lot of positive growth that one occasionally witnesses here in camp.

We never heard why our fellow camper Michael died. Did you ever hear?

Thanks again for the music cd's.

Atreus

## 9

You definitely seem to have made me something of a focus when you drop off your goodies and lead the slightly embarrassed poverty tour groups.

Here we are in Tukwila on a cow field. Seems appropriate!

Your comments, in your note, allude to my "education" and worldly experiences. You beat all around the bush rather than coming straight at me with the why are you living in this place!?

You've been a fair and generous guy the last couple of years so I'm going to share a few things with you on the whys and wherefores of my journey.

I'm a little unclear on why I'm doing this as paid professionals have tried in vain to uncork this bottle. I have the strangest feelings, only occasionally, of walking out of the water, through the damp, onto a beach I walked along a long time ago...

Sometime, before now, my heart was taken from me in a very brutal and public fashion. We were living high in our West 1 flat when she was attacked and bludgeoned to death in front of a crowd too para-lyzed to stop the insanity. Because of my "position" it was the story of the day and days and days. Without end or speculation. Everything about us was exposed to an inexhaustible scrutiny by the basest of characters.

I was so surrounded by people that I was trapped in the impossibil-ity of mourning she I had wished for, for so long. Controlled emotions in mourning, no crying, screaming or cursing God . Maintain your im-age; don't show that you're dead and waiting burial. Public mourning with a funeral that would have embarrassed her. Christ, I could hear the wallpaper peeling off. Eventually, I was told that the likelihood was that some men from the north had intentionally targeted her to strike me. They did.

Everyone kept telling me to buck up and focus on my responsibili-ties. Jesus, why didn't they just say, "move on," " put it behind you," and other ridiculous jingoism that do nothing...nothing.

Oh, there is nothing I wouldn't do to hold her again for the briefest of moments. You who dangle some fabric of hope to those of us drowning in a sea of endless blindness. What hope-more illusion. No future-just now-alone.

Long ago something broke. I have flashes of hospitals, laying in the muck, vomit, alcohol, broken bones, people looking at me in dis-gust and a long darkness warmed only by distaining eyes. A permanent daze, without a shred of care wrapped me in its snow coat.

Those were great oatmeal cookies.

# 10

Thanks for the Starbucks gift cards. Little things like that mean a lot to the people here. The note from the kids was a bonus, as often we feel forgotten in the rush of life that surrounds our bubble.

Do you ever notice how many of the people you bring to our camp look mainly towards the ground? I should talk! Well, don't bet on that, but I've noticed, from my distance, that the majority don't look too many people directly in the eyes. Do you think its fear of becoming infected with our disease? The never ebbing, ever growing, unrelenting poverty that separates and brings us together in this rag tag menagerie of hopeful and hopeless souls. Such a confusion of sounds here!

No, as far as I know, no one was ever brought to justice over my wife's death. I've been out of the light for so long I really wouldn't know if anything had developed or not. My hope is that justice rode down on them in a terrible swift moment of anguish and fear.

There were some months of activities and promises to bring justice but my unwinding and retreating into my own Coney Island took me far out of the loop.

I'm not sure if I could find my way back even if I were given hunting dogs and a map. Occasionally, I wonder if my bank accounts are real, or, misfiring neurons in a badly intoxicated fractured brain.

Please, I'm ok talking with you but I really don't want to continually relive what I went through anymore than I need to on the daily mental loop that keeps repeating...sorry, that's not very clear.

Don't make me your cause or dig into my life more than I hand you in these notes. I've found I am beginning to look forward to you coming to camp. Kind of like the fox in the Little Prince. Are you taming me? Unlikely.

I've heard we might move back to Seattle in December. Look around, this population is becoming more reflective of the mentally ill than it ever was before...I don't know if it has anything to do with being here but it is noticeable. You should hear the sounds at night! I think it reminds me of a hospital in upstate New York. Maybe not! Maybe that was somewhere else. Screaming and crying with no mother rushing to pacify. Everything will be alright, I'm here, don't cry...

Sometimes everything is not alright.

Atreus

# 11

Well, we're back in Seattle. Back to a church and its parking lot. Things are a bit different this time as we are not hidden behind the church but are located adjacent to the entrance. We had to build a wall to allow cars in and out of the lot. Looks pretty good.

It's been ok so far, considering the snow and subsequent flood that hit us on moving day. It would be nice to have some new tarps, tents, blankets and sleeping bags. I know you know. Sorry.

I heard you telling the parents, and the kids that were helping us, about the hand warmers half filled with rice and a pinch of lavender. How we heat them up for about four minutes in the microwave and then jam them into our clothes, blankets or sleeping bags. They really work! Heat radiates for hours. Apparently, those kids are going to make us a bunch for Christmas as a class project. I also heard you talking about organizing Christmas carols. I appreciate that though I look to the season with mixed feelings of muted joy and dread.

You're right; I was gone from the camp for a couple of weeks. I'm a little confused about exactly what happened so I'll convey what the cops told me before they tossed me in the tank and what the lawyer told me in the hospital. My composure and failure to meet the jailhouse dress and hygiene code lead to my ass being kicked by some easily offended cellmates. In addition to some dental work, brought on by my punchingbagness, I got a private cell with a new set of clothes. The trustee who took my clothes was wearing a hazmat outfit, well, almost. Getting hosed off in a cell isn't quite what its cracked up to be....can't be dirty in jail, you know.

A school near camp offered some gift cards to a couple of coffee shops in the big mall in, or near, Tacoma. I needed to get out of the endless rain so I went along with a few other campers. The school provided transportation in their mini van so it all looked containable.

I was wandering around the mall looking at all the things I once owned when I saw my wife. I know now, and, I guess, then, that she wasn't my wife though she was at the moment. I felt my stomach and chest constrict as I followed behind her wondering if I were in some alternate reality where none of the years existed. Was I suffering alone in my head when in fact she was all right -was I having a stroke in Harrods as I wandered behind her Christmas shopping for our friends. The food halls all looked familiar. I was having a hard time breathing. I needed to get her attention before I fell on the floor dead as a mackerel in front of the fish displays. Didn't Harrods advertise birth to death services? Maybe she could buy me a coffin upstairs? I was told I reached out for her spinning her abruptly around as I screamed some

26

incomprehensible babble. You can guess the results brought on by concerned citizens. Where were they when she really needed them?

Definitely wasn't a stellar day.

Who knows what combinations of pharmaceuticals were pumped into my veins. I still feel slightly off balance though I didn't share that with the arm crossed, frowning, anxious, apprehensive medicos who were so alarmed about my heinous behavior. I wish I could remember what I was trying to tell her.

I got it together enough to tell them some whopper about having hit my head days before in a fall in camp. It was hard as the drugs were pushing and pulling me in various directions as I tried to steer through the bog.

Within days a hospital lawyer, accompanied by a couple of shrinks, read me the riot act with warnings of dire consequences should I ever accost a citizen again. In a mall no less. How embarrassing! Dante didn't have a clue the levels one can sink to…

More than you wanted to know, huh.

I need to sleep and perhaps dream of the playing fields of Eton.

# 12

Christmas, yet again.

Thanks to you and your friends the Christmas party was a great gift to those of us who were here.

That the school would bring its choir loaded with gifts was much more than any of us could have expected. Obviously you passed on the word about hand warmers. I snagged two sets of hand warmers to keep my bag warm. I was also devious enough to grab a couple of the blankets to cushion my ride on the milk containers.

Those little kids dancing as they finished off the tree was worth the price of admission. Oh, yeah, no price other than being here.

You working on your karma account? You should have a pretty good balance by now. Kidding aside, all of you made a huge impact on the mood and timbre of the camp. I listened to a number of people talking about how they might reach out to their families for help in getting out of here.

I wish I knew where to turn. I remember so many Christmas's full of tradition, camaraderie, balls, decorations, stacks of cakes and meats fortified by ridiculously expensive cognac and wines. Man, when you're up there never seems to be a down in the path.

Once we had about fourteen carriages to roam us around the Windsor Great Park before invading the Sail Pub just down the lane for the St. George Gates. To see the castle with decorations is to glimpse the past, present and future.

It's too cold to cry.

Thanks for helping out.

Atreus

# 13

I appreciate your offer to help. I didn't intend to solicitanything from you by my last meanderings through Christmases past.

What do you mean by help? How could you help? I've been watching you for a couple of years and I'm not sure that you've got everything so tightly wound around a good plan. Are you looking for some kind of forgiveness here?

I am not your project!

Ok, sorry about that...I've started and stopped this scribbling a bunch of times as I can't seem to focus on what I want to say or whether or not I want to say anything.....

Cops were here last night. At first I thought they were coming for me for my crime wave in the mall. When I glimpsed them I shagged it outa here as fast as I could muster. I hiked down near the high school that's being remolded to get confronted by some kids who definitely didn't want "Mr. Stinky pants' walking on their turf. I took some exception to the salutation but my pants probably broadcast more than I'd like on a given summers day.

I replied with a universal hand gesture that might rank up there with some of the dumbest things I've ever done. A couple of them started bobbing and weaving in a menacing fashion shouting all sorts of Anglo-Saxon terms at me as they threatened to carve me up.

I guess I was not as appetizing as their Christmas goose. They must have reckoned I was too filthy to touch, so, a few well-placed kicks sent me on my merry way.

Had they only known how tenuous their young lives were in my hands they might have given me safer passage. Too much mindless violence.

As camp seemed to be a safer place than the streets I got back there as fast as I could. The cops were cuffing a man and woman who were stretched out across the hood of two cruisers. There were three other squad cars anticipating a riot of homeless people, I guess.

When the cops left I listened to all sorts of reasons why they were here. Rumors that the couple were robbers, illegal immigrants, car thieves etc

Another night.

I like the way your dog lays her head on my leg.

# 14

Man, its getting cold! Yes, sleeping bags and cots would be a great help. Sleeping on these milk containers is ok though its hard not to tip over if one rolls around in their sleep. Using cardboard or blankets as a mattress works pretty well. Some use second sleeping bags to ward off the cold circulating beneath. Too bad we can't have a fire in a barrel to hover around.

The church opened their recreation center for our use and warmth. Someone hooked up a television. Almost homey!

I listened attentively to your group address the camp about helping with jobs and finding places to live outside of camp.

You might understand the following but let me share it with you anyway.

Some here wouldn't know what to do with themselves if they closed a door behind themselves in an apartment. This may be grim but it offers more to some than the best of small apartments could give them at the best of times. Once they are alone in their place what are they suppose to do then? They can't tolerate being alone. Alone invites death. Death through drugs, grog, or worst of all - loneliness and isolation.

Are you going to be able to offer community in these apartments? Medical and mental support? Drugs? Support with job search. More importantly, support on the job...do you realize how many of these people don't know the first thing about how the system operates, functions or affects them...these are people outside the store window looking in to the cornucopia of unattainable treasures.

As much as you hang around I'm not sure you know the depth of anguish and fear that lives, and cries out, behind the bagels and free coffee.

Maybe you need to do something else.

# 15

My apologies. I should have known you had some insight into the challenges here. I was getting caught up in my "righteous indignation" and stepping all over myself.

I agree with everything you said - sorry that I cant seem to come out long enough to say anything back to you. These notes have become more important then I ever could have imagined. I was wondering what I would do if you didn't come round any more. That is an uncomfortable thought as I have become used to you and actually enjoy our relationship. It is a relationship, right? Am I a case study? Please say no.

I only know your first name. What if I ever wanted to reach you - what would I do? I don't like these circumlocutions. Why would I ever want to reach you? I wouldn't.

I'm not sure how I could help you? Do I appear to you as someone who could play some role in your scheme? You've seen how I hide..what are you taking about? This isn't making any sense.

Being a mute gives me the highest wall in the kingdom to stay behind.  What could you possibly do to bring things right again...don't drop bread on the water....stay away from where you don't belong as its contagious and dangerous in here.

The sweater and hat are beautiful. I can see you jestingly sauntering down the street in your Donegal tweeds.

Thanks.

# 16

I'll think about it.

The other night there was a brawl involving two guys fighting over the potential favors of a new lady in camp. Cops rolled busting the two guys. One cop started asking everyone in sight for ID. That struck fear into a number of people until one of the old timers spoke up telling the Nick that the residents didn't have to carry ID. The cop seemed determined and they squared off elevating their voices until a second squad car rolled up and the Sergeant, in that car, intervened backing off the patrolman. Peace returned to our valley.

Roy, the old timer, impressed me as he stays to himself. He hardly ever partakes in reindeer games. He's been floating around the system for years and seemingly knows every way to maneuver through whatever bureaucracy he needs to deal with. He seems as content with his place here as anywhere else he might be.

After the donnybrook, the aforementioned maiden brought Roy a cup of tea and a couple of day old donuts in thanks for standing up to

37

the heat. He got a number of nice high fives for backing down "the man." Made me laugh as the man is the thin veil that protects us from the mob that would scatter us to the wind.

If the public only knew what people say about us and why we should be shuttled off to rehab, etc.

I don't know, maybe they are right. Maybe we are a blight that should be moved for our own good to some place far from the children's eyes...

"Have they closed down the poor houses?"

Someone tossed a bunch of firecrackers over our plastic wall last night. Caused no end of panic for a few. We've picked up a few more Vets lately. Not sure what their stories are but they don't look good at all.

Please don't pressure me by repeating the same questions.

Please don't. Ok.

# 17

I'm not real sure I understand your question about food. As you can see we have piles of bread, donuts, bagels, sweet rolls, bananas, oranges and a bunch of apples.

If you're asking about the nutritional value of a diet dependent on "junk" food I think the answer should be obvious. As with most people we need protein to keep the ole noodle firing on full capacity. Well, some do, that is…some live on bread. One of the campers was talking about being a vegetarian, right, one that doesn't like vegetables. I tell you this place is full of crazier people than the institutions I've frequented!

Your group has furnished lots of meals the last few months. That a restaurant is delivering a meal every two weeks is pretty amazing. I heard that the Gourmet Grub people were homeless once. Is that true that they won a lottery and cook for shelters every week? Hmmm, food for thought!

Asking whether or not we could somehow organize ourselves into playing a contributory role in our plight is perhaps over the top. I listened to you pled with the campers when you were here about assisting you guys. Handing out thank you notes to people who have delivered stuff, that you have printed, seems more of a challenge than this place can muster. You have to understand that no one really trains anyone on the desk beyond here's the stuff and "good luck." Sometimes I feel like screaming! God, if I opened my mouth it would shock a lot of people. I came close to joining in when you were pitching the mob the other night. I wonder if I've had a stoke or something.

The campers here don't seem to realize that there is a segment of the population that think we probably deserve the life style that you see here. I agree that the camp should play a role on presenting a different face to the public than the babble I hear when some are giving tours to interested people.

I don't know if I already said this….I don't have a Xerox machine here to keep track of what I've given you…anyway, one day there was a woman taking a tour with some kids from some private school. They were wearing some snappy looking uniforms and were delivered in an XJ12 Jag making me think they probably had some dough. The driver remained in the car so I don't know if he was an actual driver or a reluctant visitor. During a conversation with Maggie, a poor mirror of a former self, she told the lady that yes indeed we needed more coffee. Maggie then went on to suggest the brand and quantity. I have not seen the woman or the Jag since though they may have come by for a drive by drop off. Can you believe it. We have the only homeless people in the country that are Vegan!!

No, I don't know what to do with all the leftover stuff. Too bad we cant figure out a way to turn it into some money, script, trade or some instrument for barter.

Let me think about this. In a previous incarnation I dealt with false currencies...

Are you roping me in? Careful. Thanks for letting me walk your dog. What's her name?

# 18

I'm glad you guys were here the other night to hear all the conflict that exists here. Bob may oversee 16 shelters but he doesn't have a clue about how to interact with this mob.

Theoretically, we are a self-governed group "hiring" Bob and that organization to manage the affairs of camp. He is suppose to get new camp sites, rent the trucks, pay for the sanicans, keep a phone in the office and give out a bus ticket per day. The truth is that he is like a British Overseer kicking putrid potatoes in the fields of Ireland. He doesn't give a wit about the growth, health, and development of anyone here. He cares about the use of us as political tools for whatever his purpose is within the overall homeless support communities. All those organizations that exist in a symbiotic relationship with us the bottom feeders.

It is outrageous that he pushed hard for us to go downtown and join people protesting the cops sweeping through greenbelts to roust people camping on public land. Did I say public land? Is that like the

British school system where private means public and vice versa? A pub versus a civilized gentleman's club, like Boodles. Had a few gins there, once...

Anyway, why should we go protest at City Hall? Are we the poster children Bob wants to use in order to elicit support from the "greater community." He's nuts! Show the public a bunch of homeless protesting and you're sure to garner support! I don't think so...

How many times have you asked the group to play a role by thanking people, cleaning up in the neighborhood, putting on a barbeque, volunteering to help out in the community. Sure we walk guard duty at camp and environs but wouldn't you think it would be more effective to have some genial folk doing those chores. Not me, for sure.

Sage. Is she named after the herb? More likely because she is wise. You may have more going for you than your bleeding heart.

# 19

I think I might have been ranting a bit when talking about Bob and our role in his politics. I don't remember exactly what I said but I should say that a lot of us would be in a world of hurt if this camp didn't exist. I can't imagine having to line up at the overnight shelters. I'd never be on time or willingly give them any particulars to muster in with the other people vying for a spot in a dorm. The tents aren't the greatest but we have coming and going privileges, minimal responsibilities, usually enough food, thanks to you guys, a TV and a group mentality that seems to shore up the weakest links in the pond.

Maybe, most importantly, we have in and out privileges that allow people to leave their swag here as they go to work, doctors appointments or all the other places people seem to disappear to on a daily basis.

We're told that the majority of campers have jobs. Maybe that's true though I never see anyone lugging in goods, other than the occasional bottle, snacks etc. If they are working it doesn't show by any shared booty with the rest of us. I'm not saying they should share any-thing. Just, that sometimes it seems that many are looking for hand outs rather than sharing. Here I am being critical of people living like I do…

If I give you a name and address could you see if it's current with-out jumping out of your clogs in excitement over me sharing and asking for a favor. Huh, a favor. Asking someone to do something for no other reason than stoking his or her generous nature.

You've probably concluded that I don't want you sharing anything with anyone if I give you a name and address - right.

# 20

I'm reconsidering you making any calls; my confidence is shaky on what you might want to blurt out. You didn't hide your enthusiasm very well and that makes me a little shaky!

Maybe I'll have to learn how to surf the Web! There was someone here the other day with a gaggle of social worker types that was pounding away endlessly on his computer. After a bit he was showing a couple of campers how they could look for job listings on the computer. I'll give the guy the benefit of the doubt that he knows we aren't packing around laptops as we dumpster dive. I've slid low but other than sleeping in a dumpster one night I've never eaten from one. At least I don't think I have!!

So, reign back your stallion on checking up on an address for me. Maybe I'll stroll on down to the local library and learn how to surf - sounds kinda fun.

I think it would be interesting to help you compile some stories from here. Stories about how people were able to change and move on...I like it. I am as invisible here as anywhere else I go, so, I might jot down what I hear and pass it on...

Those little girls sure were cute as they passed out hugs to everyone in sight. Innocence is priceless.

That's funny that the church kids thought we all lived in one big tent. I enjoy that they left assured that we weren't all crazy "like the people downtown!" We know those street people are loony!!!

Isn't it funny how we are portrayed? I mean, I've seen some stuff here, but for the most part, the people I've encountered are wandering in their inability to manage a route out. They don't really know how to approach the system or to analyze whether their perspective has any bearing on reality.

What's that ole saying," The Universe is the Illusion that sustains all Reality?"

Bring Sage back for a visit.

# 21

You're right. I am feeling better. I'm not sure exactly what's going on but I do feel engaged and a bit more at peace. Could it be the drugs???!

A fellow came the other night to camp out that caused no end of desolation. The poor guy had sustained an injury in Afghanistan that left a good part of the left side of his face a mess. His left leg seems to have been injured as well. I have the distinct feeling he was loaded on something way stronger than the Jack that was wafting off him. Can't say I blame him…

People forgot whatever was on their agendas and reached out in ways I haven't seen here before. A couple of ladies took him in tow for a meal as an area was cleaned out for a private tent. For inexplicable reasons the camp waved the necessity of staying in the men's tent for a month. Not so inexplicable.

He was gone in the morning. I was going to talk with him.

I recall a poor jarhead that stepped out of the M13 to "get the beer." Poor bastard stepped on a mine losing most of his right leg, genitals, lower arm and the majority of his face. We evacuated him and spun two AC-47's around the perimeter to saturate the place with the breath of the dragon. Believe it or not he lived. I lost track of how many surgeries he survived. I last saw him in London. He was--------

I heard he died. Poor guy.

I don't remember if I told you or not that we were getting more veterans in here. I think our visitor was the only fellow that had seen combat. I don't know what to think about it. Would any group of people have a certain percentage that was malfunctioning? Are people in homes loaded on whiskey and drugs really much different than the souls collected on this island? Are Priests, Rabbis, Mullahs, showgirls, soccer moms, insurance sales people, bankers etc any more balanced than we are? I'll give you they are functioning better but I'm willing to risk that they may not be all that much different than a lot of us.

I'm getting tired of this…the noise at night is too much.

## 22

Where you been? I don't think I've seen you in weeks.

I went to the library to see what I could find out about the "super hi-way." Boy, I've been off the chart for longer than I thought. I felt like Rip Van Winkle when I asked the information lady about how to surfboard. I wore the sweater and snappy hat you gave me giving me quite the debonair airs. That she laughed when I asked about surfboarding took a small slice out of my starch but I felt a little too good to be bush wacked. Back at camp there was a bottle of Old Spice up by the EC's desk which I took advantage of before my adventure. I might have put too much on as I was getting eyes on the bus. I'll admit it's vile but I needed to be spruced up...

Did you know you can look up addresses on the computer? The lady told me you can google names. I didn't have a clue so she showed me how to do it. When she walked away I put my name in the box though nothing showed up. Good to know I'm not in that system. Maybe I should check the obituaries? Maybe you could help me get a library card as the lady said I needed one if I want to use the computers again.

There is a shrink that is offering his services to the camp for free. He talked about strategies rather than fixing any of us. Made a good pitch and brought a hell of a dinner to boot. Maybe I'll sign up. Made you smile, huh!

Yea,'67, Operation Cedar Falls. You think we're crazy? You should have had a few beers with more than one tunnel rat at a time.

I wasn't in the military so your idea or using Veteran's care isn't an option. Thanks for checking it out. Doesn't apply.

Hard to imagine how cold it is here. Freezing in the tents at night. I heard some guy brought in a little propane heater to warm up his tent. It got confiscated moments after he fired it up. Hell of an argument followed with him getting barred for a month.

The extra blankets will help.

# 23

I don't know, I just haven't felt like writing much lately.

Seems like a long road down for all of us.

I suppose you heard what happened the other night across the street? Hard to believe I live in a major 1$^{st}$ world city that has its people dying on the streets. Sweet Jesus, where is Mother Theresa when we need her!

Somewhere around three in the morning I awoke to a lot of voices and horrendous screaming coming from over by the church. By the time I got across the street there was a crowd of campers around a woman on the ground screaming bloody murder. One of our guys was ministering to her in a very appropriate way. The desk guys apparently called 911 but no help in sight when I got over there...

There was blood everywhere. I couldn't tell from my vantage point what may have happened to her but I could see her right wrist was bent in an unnatural way. All of a sudden she went quiet. Our guy started mouth to mouth. Within moments a fire truck arrived followed by a couple of cop cars. Those guys did all sorts of things including hitting her with the jumpers. In the midst of all this they were complimentary to our camper, turns out his name is Gregor, on how he took charge and did everything just right. They told him that if he had more time, and got there earlier, she might have survived. Dam shame.

Cops made us all stick around telling them everything we knew or thought we knew. I walked as far away as possible from the campers when one cop started asking me questions. I knew if I clammed up I'd be downtown or back in some wacky ward awaiting whatever joys those guys might bring my way. Taking the easier route I told the flick everything I knew, which was nothing. It was interesting to hear my own voice. I sounded remarkably coherent. Hmmm.

About a week later Bob came to camp and told us he had heard she was murdered. She was pregnant. Only 17 years old with a record of drug use and the sale of drugs.

I don't understand what we're doing anymore.

## 24

Thanks for the kind words and flowers. I haven't gotten flowers since before I can remember. My wife occasionally sent flowers to my office just for the love of it.

I guess I wasn't paying enough attention to my health as a cold went south on me directly into my lungs. I feel a little ashamed of my hermit like behavior. I could have descended into the depths if everyone here was more like me. Fortunately, for me, there are enough busy bodies here that an aid car was called and I was taken to Harborview pretty much against my will. My will! Like a salmon wills to swim up stream!

Couples of days in hospital have me back in form. Don't worry that you couldn't visit. I very much realize you have a life, light years from here. Your card and flowers were unexpected and welcomed. You are a good guy…don't lose it.

Remember I told you about Gregor and how he helped the kid that died across the street. OK, get ready for this - I talked to him later for a few minutes. Turns out he was an EMT with the Billings fire department. He told me one of the firemen gave him his business card and asked him to call if he needed anything. He told me he was going to call him and see if there was anything he could do with the department here. After a really long period of silence he told me he had to get out of here or he was going to destroy himself. I didn't say anything. He told me to get out before this became my life. If he only knew! If I only knew how long I've been wondering.

I've got a few stories for you on some campers.

What are you going to do with them?

Do you keep the notes I give you? I may want them back one of these days, ok?

## 25

Did I tell you that we recently got invited by the girls school down the street to attend a church service with them? Well, we did, and, I did. At first it felt kind of funny to be in a church considering how many times I've dammed God for his lack of attention. Maybe I need to be a little more forgiving and say a prayer for God. Pray that he gets his focus back! Don't worry, I feel confident he isn't listening to my rambles. I'll be all right.

It turns out the church is a Jesuit parish. I didn't know they had parishes and I am proud to say how much respect I have for them for the way they turned the ship of state during the reformation. Never mind!

The priest was joined by a Rabbi and an Episcopal priest to celebrate the "day of giving." That was the theme that probably prompted the girls to extend an invitation to the campers. Whatever the motivation it was it was nice to be included.

I wish I had encountered a priest like this guy years ago. He seemed to have put his ego on hold. He had spent a number of years working on a reservation as well as street work in San Francisco. He definitely knew what he was talking about.

"Marginalized people living on the border of acceptability." I would say acceptability was a stretch at times. Sometimes I wonder if we would be physically driven away if the thin wall of the law were punctured by wider unrest.

The girls sang like angels. It was funny how they tried to get those of us attending to play an interactive role with them during the service. Maurice, who is always singing in camp, took full advantage of the occasion and bellowed out like a bull moose. Actually, he's got a great singing voice that was roundly appreciated by everyone in the church. Lots of laughs and hugs from the kids who truly want to help us do something with our lives. I think they are all way too young to realize some of us aren't going anywhere anytime soon.

I hope their innocence wraps around them forever.

The Rabbi and minister were great additions fully supporting all of us in society challenged in all ways imaginable. We were all invited to take part in communion but I didn't want to push my luck with that trespass!

After the service we all went into the community hall for coffee, tea and a shot at more donuts than I've ever seen balanced in a single pile before...

The little church ladies produced a breakfast suitable for a lumberjack. Eggs, flapjacks, bacon, sausage, ham, potatoes, cornbread, muffins, pounds of butter and jam. It was right up there with the most memorable breakfasts I've ever had - didn't have to pay for it either.

58

There is a shelter downtown that charges admission to their meals - you have to sit through an hour of "get your life together" spiel. I did that once and it was once too many times.

Towards the end of the meal the kids gave each of us a little package full of toiletries. What a nice thing to do. Its funny that we get tons of bread and lots of care products…hmmm. Each package also included a hand drawn picture and a happy note. Maybe God is on point!

Father Jim (when did they start going by their first names?) came around our table offering an open invitation to any of us who would like to join him for dinner and a game of cards any Thursday night.

I can't tell you how good that felt. I'm going to do it though I don't know exactly why I feel so excited by the prospect.

Bring Sage around.

# 26

Did I ask you about my notes?  I get the feeling that I'm repeating myself and I don't want to be redundant.  Did you know that when you're on the dole in the U.K. you receive a cheque that has "redundancy pay" written right on the cheque! As if being out of work isn't enough of an insult.

What was it I was going to tell you?  I have a stack of note cards to pass along.  Maybe I should get a spiral note pad and start dating things I give you, well, maybe not. Seems way too organized and too much like a previous style.

Now I remember. I was, am, going to share Maria and Vic's story. You are still interested in "collecting" stories, right?

There were very few people sitting around camp so I felt pretty at ease asking Maria if she'd mind sharing her story with me.  I told her you were going to do something with them to fund raise and that you had assured me no real names would be used.  Did I make that up or did I actually tell me that? If I made it up I hope you are clever enough to keep all of us out of the direct light. I mean, who knows what is true and what is a rationalization for living like a encumbered gypsy...

Maria is from Abilene, Texas. I'd guess she is about forty. Woman are tough to guess the age of when they're looking their best, when they look beat down it adds a lot of unnecessary years. That she smokes like a chimney doesn't help.

She told me she finished high school but doesn't feel she really learned anything. Her interests were outside of school, mainly around the need to have boys like her. She didn't really say how well that worked out for her but she did refer to two kids that live with her aunt and uncle. I didn't catch where they are and didn't feel it was my business to ask.

When she was mid twenties she fell in love and married a long hauler who was gone most of the time. Her ideal marriage didn't live up to her dream, so they separated.

(I felt real good talking with her, like I might be able to say something that might matter to someone. I've been in here a long time by myself)

She moved to the Dakotas, Kansas, New Mexico making a living waiting tables. She really liked Taos.

I asked her why she kept moving. All I got in reply was a shake of her head.

A couple of years ago she moved to Portland and then about a year ago to Seattle. She was waiting tables trying to save enough dough to get a better apartment than the one she had and to give herself the ability to dream about her kids. I don't know why but I get the impression both kids aren't actually hers. I asked but didn't get a clear answer. She was getting kinda spooky with her answers. I didn't want to ruin my maiden voyage into being your cub reporter so I took it easy with the questions.

About five months ago she got the flu. She didn't have any insurance or enough in the bank to cover what became strep and something else she didn't identify. She seemed shamed to have gone repeatedly to emergency rooms, as she got sicker. She told me she thumbed her way to Everett so no one would know her at the local emergency room. When she got to the hospital in Everett they admitted her for whatever complications she didn't want to mention. Well, the short story is she was in hospital for 17 days where she nearly died. Transfusions and emergency surgery have indebted her for the foreseeable future. She said she gave her true name but didn't list any relatives, as she didn't want them going after them for any money. She wants to payoff the hospital but has no idea how to accomplish that feat.

When she got out of the hospital she found a pay or vacate letter in her apartment. She had missed the previous months rent and now was looking at a figure that was beyond her reach. The manager told her he had a couple waiting to move in should she not be able to come up with the rent. She told him she was getting a check from work and would have it caught up in a week's time. She went to the restaurant where she worked to be told she had been replaced and that there were no open positions. She got a few minutes with the day manager who told her she should have notified them she was taking time off. He added chocolate to the cake by saying he could not give her a positive reference. I think she went on a bit of a jag for a time as she made a couple of asides to hanging out in the Globe tavern, a historic den of questionable repute.

After some amount of time she spoke with a Real Change newspaper salesman who gave her the skinny on where to apply for help and how she could get shelter with no money. After a couple of indoor shelters she realized she could live here in a tent with the freedom to hustle a new job, saving everything she makes weekly. She feels bad she split her apartment under a lie and wants to give the landlord the past rent. I wonder if she realizes how unique she is with that position.

You wouldn't think it possible but she met Vic right here in our encampment.

Vic is from the Chicago area. He's lived all over making a few bucks here and there as a guard, taxi driver, Mr. fixit and a few other pursuits. From what Maria says they hit it off right away. He is driving for the cab company that is owned by Sikhs. She said they have a program to reach out to people in need and that Vic was real lucky to have heard about their program and to get hired almost immediately from when he went to talk with them. I forgot to mention that Maria is working at a Denny's down by the wharf (She likes it a lot).

Maria spoke to the Reverend who comes here all the time. You know her. The lady that always brings warm food and socks for most of us. I guess that minister's church has a matching fund thing that is going to allow Maria and Vic an opportunity to get an apartment within weeks. They will match what Maria and Vic save and make the

64

arrangements with the new landlord. She thinks the arrangement is with Catholic Relief but she's not sure - just happy.

I didn't get a chance to talk with Vic. Is this what you're looking for? I feel like Jimmy Olson waiting for Mr. White to give him a pat on the head.

Be sure to file my story above the fold!!!!!

Atreus

Camp Reporter

# 27

This neighborhood is becoming a shooting gallery!

Yesterday afternoon someone walked into the Cajun place up the street and opened fire. One guy was killed and two people were injured as they tried to bail out the window ....cops all over the place.

The heat rolled in looking in every tent to see who was here. From what we could gather, from listening to the radio chatter, they are looking for an Asian kid. Well, they're actually pretty shaky on that as the descriptions were varied, according to the regular beat cop. He's a nice guy and always has something nice to say to everyone when he stops by camp. He's always promoting jobs he's seen that may be of interest to any of us. Occasionally he brings homemade pies.

Cops were really nervous. One of our guys chose their visit as his time to rant about coming fascism and the loss of all our rights. I don't think he realized just how nervous the cops were or he might have kept his mouth shut. One cop got in his face enough to get him to back down and keep quite.

When all the smoke cleared I spoke to Sammy. He's the one that riled the cops with his political insights. Sammy seems to live in two places simultaneously. He is here and in that other place, switching back in forth in a blink within a sentence. At moments it was like looking in the mirror.

Anyway, take the following with a grain of salt, as I have no idea what is fact and what is of the dream world.

Sammy is probably early thirties. He looks older but that could be due to whatever lifestyle he's been living more than the numbers on a calendar.

Sammy says he's from Carson City. He was born and raised there remaining until he was in his mid twenties. He was a dealer at the Nugget casino where he said he had the happiest times of his life. He told me he got in some trouble leading him to a stretch in the state pen in Carson. (Add in a bunch of nonsense babble about the mayor and governor I sat through before he got back on planet.)

Since he was a con he couldn't work in the casinos anymore. He looked for work with little luck. He teamed up with a fellow con to do some day labor jobs, which kept food on the shelves. This friend had a friend who ran two boats out of Westport. Sam agreed to head north and give fishing a try, as it didn't look like anything was going to pop in Nevada.

If I understand the rest of his story correctly he came up to Westport and learned the ropes of being a deckhand. Seems all was going well until the day he got tossed overboard miles out on a halibut fish. The sea was so rough it took about fifteen minutes to get him back in the boat. Apparently, he was unconscious and suffering from hypothermia when they hooked him back on the boat. They actually had to use one of their gaffes as he was beginning to sink. Within an hour the Coast Guard sent out a chopper to transport him to a hospital back in Westport. According to Sammy he incurred some brain damage, as he was actually dead for a few of the minutes he was in the ocean. He kept coming back to how the bastards had used a gaffe on him like he was a "flounder". I didn't want to argue the point.

He told me the shrink that visits camp is going to get him transferred to a home where he can get some rehabilitation services. I am not real clear on how he sees moving on but it would be good for him if he had someone keeping a more caring eye on him than can be done around here. Having been a guest of the mental institutional system I'd go for the home in a second.

# 28

I know it's been a while since I've given you any of my scribbling. Just don't use my name. I don't think you know it anyway, do you? No, I am ok with you putting it all together.

Remember the shooting I told you about. The one in the restaurant. Our local cop was here the other day and told us they thought it was a gang initiation. They haven't caught anyone yet.

Can you believe it! Kill someone to get in a gang. I thought I'd seen the worst but this may be the ultimate. How empty do you have to be to want some petty recognition so much that you kill someone without any concern, remorse, or heart!? I can't remember when I've been so angry.

Yes I do. She never leaves my mind. There every second glancing back at me as she retreats further and further away.

I went over to the priests house the other night. I thought, from hearing people around here talking, that there would be a crowd. Nope, just me. I would have preferred to stay on the ropes with other people doing all the talking even though I've been practicing my oral skills recently. Once I rang the doorbell I was condemned.

He is a great guy, Father Jim. I told him I couldn't call him just Jim and he seemed to be ok with hearing the Father title every time I addressed him. I think his twinkle is as much internal as external...

We had a nice dinner with him telling tales of living with the Sioux near the Rosebud res. Interesting that he seemed to acknowledge my reluctance to play a major speaking role. I gained a lot of respect for his insight. I was going to duck out the door immediately after the meal but he convinced me to try a hand of cards. I think the offer of cognac might have played a role in my decision to stick around.

Have you ever heard of a game called "Punto'? An Italian game that is suited for two players. Its really fast and fun. We had some good laughs, mainly at my expense.

I was tempted to open conversation, but, something held me back.

In about an hours time he offered me a ride which I declined. I preferred to re ground walking back through the neighborhood. A door out?

# 29

Before I go back to something I meant to tell you I want to tell you about "Big Jim."

I'm sure you know him, or, knew him. He's been gone for a few weeks.

A while ago he took advantage of a class that was offered the camp by some volunteer group. They offered to pay for and transport anyone who was interested in getting their servers card. I think that's what it was called; anyway, it was basic training on hygiene and how to operate in a kitchen. Nice offer for anyone interested in that work.

One of the trainers got to talking to him and after determining that Jim had done some basic prep work in a kitchen he told Jim to apply for an opening at the restaurant where the trainer worked.

Well, you'll recall that Jim was as big as a doublewide Winnebago.

Fortunately for Jim, he said something about not having the proper clothing to wear to an interview to his trainer. Here's where the miracle happens. The training guys daughter is in a Camp Fire club (I don't know what you call a mob of Camp Fire girls?). No, her being in campfire isn't the miracle. Its that he and his daughter appealed to the club, parents and sponsors who stepped up to take Jim to J.C.Penny's to get him two complete outfits including underwear, socks and shoes. Can you believe it!

Pretty nice, huh.

It gets slightly better. Jim got hired at a fair rate with benefits kicking in within 180 days if everything works out ok for everyone. Maybe the best is that he can use the small apartment above the restaurant. He had to agree to some additional security responsibilities etc to get that perk.

Good luck Jim!!

# 30

Well, the angel of death rode through here last night. This visit comes on the heels of the last death a little too quickly for my peace of mind.

A young lady, Karin, no more than mid twenties, went into convulsions about 10:15. A group of us were in the big tent watching a movie the pastor from across the street brought over for our amusement.

I wasn't sitting near her so some of what I'm sharing is what others said later on when everything was concluded. Apparently everything was just fine until she mentioned to her friend that her ear was really hurting. A couple of seconds after saying that she tumbled out of her chair into a Grand Mal on the ground. A couple of people rushed her to help. I couldn't see what was going on as others blocked me view. Lots of shouting for an aid car.

The fire department must have been down the street because they appeared, literally, within minutes.

They asked us to give them room and offer the young lady some privacy. From my vantage point I could see how serious and frantic they became once they got her vitals. They tried everything including the paddles. It wasn't long before it became obvious to all of us that she had dropped her body and moved on...

The silence in camp was measurable. Everyone who was in camp, stood around, not knowing what to do or say to anyone. It was like we were all looking down our own private roads to the same old decrepit hotel in the distance.

The fireman who was working on Karin the most had tears running down his cheeks. It really moved me to see how he was affected by this stranger's death. I wonder why?

The cops showed up, along with the blackened windowed wagon to take her to God knows where. A cold and lonely place I'm sure...

The police had to do their thing inclusive of asking all of us everything we knew. Only her friend had any information and that was sliver thin.

They apologized when they entered Karin's tent to gather her belongings. I guess they were going to determine whatever they could from what they had to examine.

After way too long the poor soul was put in a black plastic bag to be moved into the van. A couple of campers went up to the gurney to give her a touch before she disappeared forever. It was quite the scene.

A couple of cops hung around to have coffee with us. Not much was being said by anyone. Each person was wherever he or she was with Karin's death.  That the cops would hang around gave me a great sense of belonging to something bigger than our shoddy tent city.

Dawn was breaking in spite of my desire to stay comfortable in the night.

# 31

Last night seems to have taken a toll on the whole camp. Thoughts of health, family, loneliness and the specter of dying amid strangers in a transient camp probably weigh heavily on some. I know its bothering me. This is no longer an end to a means...you know what I mean.

The "Ladies in Black" arrived mid afternoon to begin their silent vigil in respect to Karin's death. I guess I'd heard about them but never really focused on who or what they were all about. They go to the site of a homeless persons death to stand silently to draw attention to the fact that we are people and not a disposable to be kicked under a rusting car sitting at the curb.

In my wildest nightmares I never could have imagined being in the situation I find myself in at the moment. I've come to realize that so many people I have not interacted with have passed through here without a glimpse from me. Strangers who because of their generosity have kept us whole during all sorts of crisis and challenges supported them. I could have done more. I should have done more. She would be ashamed of me and how I've wrapped myself in such a self destructive way. I always wanted her to be proud of me. I would do anything to have her love deepen. She was my whole point of existence. If she can in fact watch me on this plane I am so sorry, sorry I'm weak and sorry I cant seem to see how to move from this spot. Please forgive me and give me some help to do something, anything different than this…

# 32

I've been roaming around the shelter system for a few weeks. I needed to get out of here for a while.

There seems to be no end to the amount of people who are wandering around looking for a place to eat, drink, or sleep. I don't know, but, it appears to me that the homeless population is growing. Maybe I'm just seeing it with slightly different eyes.

I stayed in an outdoor shelter across the lake for about a week. They have figured out how to make their situation much more comfortable than we have here. My first impression is that there are fewer people over there dealing with mental issues than here. A lot of residents have cars, flower pots in front of their tents and an attitude to get up and get out that doesn't exist in the city. Is it just the throw of the dice or does the city attract a different type of camper?

Believe it or not - you probably know this - they have a portable shower! When I spoke with any of the campers they showed a certain disdain for their city relatives in our camp. I can see why as we are low on pride and they are jamming trying to get jobs, apartments and support from lots of organizations to get them up and out. They have two meals a day and sponsor a thank you meal for all the people who have supported them in any given location.

That is a great way to increase support in the neighborhoods.

Speaking of which. The day before yesterday I joined a contingent of campers to attend a community meeting by the old Army base. We were invited to camp on a church property near there in a few months....

It was the largest gathering I've seen since I've been in this cycle. I had planned, and promised myself, that I would speak up. No way! This was an ugly crowd full of conclusions on why we would be blight on the land if allowed to camp at the church. The poor Vicar, or whatever he is, got his knickers jammed as he invited us without asking this mob of upstanding folk for permission. Some man, apparently, on some committee to end homelessness, quoted some rules and regulations allowing the church to make any decisions it wanted with its property. Man, did it go further down hill after that gauntlet was dropped.

I guess the biggest surprise and saddest thing that happened was to hear from a woman who had been homeless a number of years ago. She told how she lived in a car for a certain period of time and then how she pulled herself up by "her bootstraps" to become a successful marketing person. Whatever that is?

When she started out I thought it was going to be a great endorsement of the camp and the viability of an outdoor shelter. Was I ever wrong! She told stories of drugs, drunkenness and how she was afraid a great deal of the time that she had spent in two shelters, including ours in a former incarnation.

She won over the crowd.

The poor minister didn't know what to do so he apologized to the neighbors with the promise of a reconsideration of the extended invitation. A gray wind blew through the room.

I remember hearing a man at Speakers Corner challenge the Anglican Church with the chant, "Revere him, although, never act like him." I didn't understand at the time but I think I get it now. Where have all the courageous people gone? Doesn't it say somewhere to take care of the poor? Hmmm.

I've seen Father Jim a few times. I'll tell you about that later. Maybe.

Would you mind bringing me all the notes etc I've given you? Not sure why but I'd like to watch them burn.

One of the guys here is a twelve stepper always offering some pearl of wisdom from the "Big Book." Someday I'm going to ask to see it as the name is really bugging me. Is it really big or is that some clever metaphor?

I was half-heartedly listening to him the other day when he was telling a couple of people about going to rehab for a month. He said they required he keep a notebook current to each day's sessions of individual and group therapy. The last day of his stay he had to tell a councilor his story and why he had chosen drugs versus reality. I made that part up, as I don't know exactly what he was supposed to do…Anyway, after telling his story he was to go out to the camp grill area and burn all the notes he had taken during the month. He explained it as a letting go, self-forgiving exercise.

I am ok with whatever you have done with my notes but I would like them back. I'll make a little sacrifice and burn them tossing the thoughts to the four winds of change.

# 33

Big Jim. The guy who went to work in the restaurant was back here the other day. Looks as if he's gained some weight working in the kitchen! He brought some nice desserts and the offer of a dish-washing job to the first person that shows up to claim the position. Lets hope there is a stampede!

Do you know who Gail is? Little mousey woman who wears her troubles on her face like a salted scar?! Like me she never says a lot and keeps pretty much to herself. I figured she was a street girl though that wouldn't seem to be very productive for her in the best of times. She comes and goes sometimes returning looking as if she took a beat-ing out there somewhere. Sad little thing lost in whatever construct she has built around herself.

Her family arrived here looking for her on Tuesday.

Gail was in her tent when they approached the EC at the desk. He sent the fire watch to get her.

I was drawing a mug of coffee when this began, so, this is all first hand stuff I'm giving you. I didn't know they were family, as it's not too unusual for people to pull up and ask for someone or other...

When Gail walked up to the desk, in her usual, head down, staring at the ground style I had no idea of what was going to transpire.

At her arrival at the desk she looked up at the couple who were nervously standing there wringing their gloved hands. You could feel the air change in that visual embrace. Nothing! Not a sound, not a movement, not a stir of any kind. I was riveted in my awareness of this moment between the actors on stage.

In about forty-five seconds Gail let her head roll back towards her shoulders as she began to cry. Her arms were akimbo in total submission.

The man stepped forward engulfing her in his arms. The woman, just a split second behind the man, joined the embrace. It went on forever with the three of them openly weeping without a concern to the world spinning around them.

A few campers stood at a polite distance offering their support with kudos about sweet Gail. Eventually, Gail broke off, returning to her tent. In a few moments she returned to the couple accompanied by the smallest of bags tucked under her arm. As they were stepping back on to the sidewalk Gail turned to those of us watching saying, "These are my parents who have come to take me home. Thank you all for giving me a place to stay. You will be in my prayers every night. I will pray all your parents come and take you home."

Other than one of the campers quietly weeping there wasn't a sound to be heard.

Mom and dad, I wonder if you would have come to get me. Would you, my ghost? Have I gone too far this time?

# 34

I led a tour of camp yesterday. Ok, they were second graders from some school making it easier on me than it might have been otherwise. Cute little kids full of hope and empathy. Their teacher had prepared them very well other than them thinking this is a really cool place to live. I guess if I were in second grade this would look pretty full of adventure. Wait until they see Willie with his silver eyepiece (Actually, he wasn't in camp). They would probably think he was a pirate!

I told them about us moving every couple of months, what we watched on TV, what we ate and how we were out of doors for a number of reasons. I think I was dumbing it down too far when one little tyke mentioned most people were homeless due to money problems. Kid will probably grow up to be astronaut. Lets hope so-----

They brought us sandwiches in decorated brown sandwich bags. I guess we have peanut butter and jam, cookies, potato chips, fruit and a little box drink. The teacher said the kids collected the money to buy the supplies, made the sandwiches, decorated the bags and wrote notes to each of us hidden in the interior sandwich wrap. There <u>is</u> a God and he lives among the innocent hiding from the rest of us.

Before I forget let me tell you a little about Willie. The first thing you notice is that he's way too tall and gangly to be a pirate with a parrot on his shoulder. I always envision pirates to be mid height and strong as the tide. Willie reminds me of what Icabod Crane would look like if he weren't running for his life through the bridges of Tarrytown.

Back to the point. Willie wears an oblong engraved silver eye patch over his left eye. Your eyes are unwillingly drawn to the patch whether you want to or not...

Seems he was working as a lumberjack when one day, while buzzing his way through a tree, a chip flew back taking his eye out in a flick. Quick end to working with chain saws and falling trees. He mended fairly quickly. His fellow "jacks" didn't want to pair up with a blind guy bringing this career to a close for the time being. Willie often says he was never so happy as when he was in the forest felling trees.

The company he worked for was nice enough to give him an inside job tracking the jobs and assigning the men, and two women, to sections and responsibilities. Willie says he was having problems adjusting to reading with one eye mixed with an increase of booze and "recreational" drugs to lesson the pain in his body and mind.

One thing led to another and he was asked to move on. He was arriving at work either terribly hung over or blatantly high as a kite. He moved to Yakima to live with his younger brother and to look for work. He and his brother didn't get along for long. His brother's girl friend was/is born again and didn't want to put up with Willie's nonsense for long. Can't blame her for that...

He moved to Seattle a few months ago to find work and a place to live. He's been doing day labor every day, as far as I know, since he's been here.

Seems like things are going to change for Willie as he found out from Social Security today that there is money available for training. Since his accident took him out of his career field he can go to school, apply for reduced housing and receive benefit checks at the same time. He thinks it would be good to get a degree and maybe work for Fish and Game.

Hard to measure his happiness other than to tell you he kept repeating he felt as if someone had tossed him a life raft as he was about to go down for the third time.

Good to hear he'll be moving on - time for all of us to move on.

# 35

I mentioned I've been talking with Father Jim quite a bit, didn't I. I found when I first went over to his house that he had a knack for listening without any prejudice or recognizable agenda. I imagine his years with the Sioux taught him how to listen if he didn't have that talent before he lived with them.

It's interesting that the Jesuits send their people where they think they are needed versus the priest determining where he is going. I didn't say that very well…a Jesuit can have a high public office and find that when his term is over he might be working in a town parish, a hospital, teaching or working with some particular disadvantaged group. They take a vow of obedience, which in some ways, makes it easier than making your own destiny. Father Jim gave me a book by one of his fellow priests. I don't have it right in front of me so I'll give you the title some other time. It's by a priest who lived in Portland spending every waking minute with the street people in the downtown area. I haven't read much of it yet though I recognized a lot of familiar territory in the first few chapters. I'll probably find my unique self in the middle of the bell curve in a different city at a different time. Are we really all that different from each other?

Is my story totally mine or a compilation of my experiences and those I think I've had versus those I've really had…like when you try to remember being a little kid. Can you really remember those memories or are they imprinted from stories rather than true events in your life. Admittedly I've scrambled some time and brain cells. Been thinking a lot about what I think and feel.

# 36

You missed the Mayor and his minions visit yesterday. If anyone knew they were coming I hadn't heard about it or I would have vacated the premises.

Actually, that's a bit unfair as the Mayor took some time to look around and talk with a few of the residents. I went into the large men's tent, as I didn't want to take part in the conversation. Funny, now I wish I had said a thing or two about what might help out with this merry band of campers.

He had a cup of coffee and a couple of day old donuts with a couple of the ladies who had kitchen duty. Everyone seemed to appreciate his visit though none seemed to have any idea why he was here or what might come from the visit. There wasn't any press with him so who knows ???

It would be nice if the political forces came together to work out some solutions to how people can get into some kind of cheaper housing than seems to be available…

We're gearing up for another move in a few days. We'll be crossing the city into a neighborhood where the camp has never stayed before now. Should be interesting as the neighbors were not overjoyed at the prospect of having us near three schools and play grounds. I cant think of what can be said to offset this preconception of who we are - we are not a threat!!

It would be interesting to pull back the lace curtains in the neighborhood to see what some of those people are up to in their darkened rooms. Scary thought, huh.

Have you heard the proposal kicking around camp?

I'm not sure where it originated but the idea is to limit the amount of time one can reside here. One year is being kicked around. I'm of mixed thoughts as I've been here, off and on, for way longer than a year. The way it works now is that you can live here forever if you want to….as you know, a few of the campers aren't really homeless as this is in fact their home.

Some city or state oversight group is trying to force transition out of homelessness by demanding certain criteria be met by the residents and overseers. All organizations that support shelters would be required to offer, and be accountable for, training in every aspect of survival. Making sure people have writing and oral skills, job search, health and dental care, financial training, assistance with interview skills, job placement etc., etc., etc.

I guess we have to look at what we want in our communities. Obviously, we don't want wandering camps of homeless moving around the city in search of permanency. Did you hear my tone? "We don't want wandering camps of homeless!!!" Where did that come from?? Who am I to say anything? Ok, let me get my thoughts together.

Nothing like a walk, to clear your head. It would have been nice to have your dog pulling me around the hood.

Six months ago I couldn't find my way alone if I were required to leave this camp. Would it be fair to force others to clear out within a certain time frame? What exists here shouldn't be in a nation that prides itself on its ranking in the world. That it exists at all is an indictment of our societal priorities. All of us should have a strong net beneath us when, and if, the house of cards comes crumbling down. This is our net even if not state promoted.

That this shelter offers some security and a sense of belonging is in itself a good step up from the streets, or the more demanding shelters. This isn't easy to solve. On the one hand camp offers a lot without making great demands. Maybe the services proposed could be offered without the threat of expulsion. Have people in camp support the programs and push them more gently showing the results of stepping up towards a transition out of here.

I know certain organizations will fight whatever is proposed. I'm getting all worked up over nothing!

Sure, I'll go to coffee with you.

# 37

We had a contingent of police come to camp during our weekly meeting. They were concerned with our welfare as there have been a number of homeless targeted in certain neighborhoods.

I should have volunteered my tale of being a kicking bag but I didn't think they would appreciate my unsolicited antidotal sharing.

The cops seemed genuine in their concern for us. Interesting that they seemed so open. Maybe we are too easy a population to target. As you can guess, we the homeless are not being robbed but beaten up for being blight on the city. Not sure the perps would know what a blight is though they probably feel they are doing the public good by bashing us to smithereens. The cops told us they are certain we are targeted because we are vulnerable. They suggested we travel in twos and threes and not wander the streets alone aimlessly. Funny, we <u>are</u> aimless!

One cop kept looking at me, which I found very disturbing. Every time I looked up he was looking at me. What was he thinking? Was he involved in any of my more stellar moments? Was I caught drinking stale beer from slug traps? Throwing up into convertible Porsches?

God, did I do any of those things?

It passed.

Cops said they would increase their drive bys and assured us that we were not going to be victimized because we were experiencing tough times. They told us a community group had agreed to walk the neighborhood with us to further insure our safety. Wow. Is there no limit to what some are willing to do for us?

I am beginning to feel guilty about my role here.

I spruced myself up the other day and took a bus downtown. I wasn't the best-dressed guy down there but I certainly wasn't the worst. I found I could be invisible in the crowds surfing the tide of movement from street to street. It was enjoyable to walk around until my memories of her started to temper my enjoyment. Will I want her next to me forever? She fades in and out.

I went into the Olympic Hotel for a break. I was sure the doorman would wrestle me to the ground, or, if I cleared that hurdle I'd be bopped on the head by some wacked out security guard in the lobby. I was trespassing into the inner sanctum! Much to my amazement the door was opened for me with a greeting to enjoy my stay. My stay, what a laugh! In the old days, maybe.

I found an empty sofa and sat down as if I had a purpose in the place. No one seemed to realize a waif from the streets had infiltrated them. Everyone was milling around on one mission or another without a glimpse in my direction. Actually, the place was jumping with a mix of guests and workers interacting on all sorts of levels. After a bit I cruised the lobby stores and then headed up to the Georgian Room for a look-see. A very smart young man handed me a menu for my perusal. Funny, I had about eight bucks in my pocket, which would not have gotten me half of a cob salad. I told him I was waiting for my wife, which got the universal nod of understanding. I asked him if it was ok for me to have a coffee. Before he seated me I told him I was going to clear my account and only had a few bucks on me. Much to my surprise he said the coffee was on the house and not to be concerned about anything more than enjoying myself. Am I in Disneyland?

So, there I was sitting in the Georgian Room knocking back Honduran coffee as if I didn't have a worry in the world. Actually, I didn't have any worries.

Talking with Father Jim I shared with him how I was beginning to feel badly about disappearing without any concern for those that might care about me.

Remind me of this epistle when we have our coffee as I am beginning to get concerned about my writings and any plans you have for their sharing.

# 38

No, forget what I said about my writings. I see your point and give you my blessing to do whatever you want with them. If you can actually make any changes because of me I'd be proud to have played a role. Go ahead and transcribe them but please return them to me. Ok.

This morning a group of realtors came by to tell us about their cooperative that is considering offering studio and one-bedroom apartments to low-income people at a fair bargain. They wanted to know if we had any ideas that they might not have thought of-can you believe it?

They may be able to get a discount on their financing of construction projects if they offer a percentage towards lower income people. They seemed very open about what they were trying to do and how it would benefit them as well as people who had a hard time getting into apartments. The new idea is that they would try to get the state to allow their support payments to be applied towards a down payment thereby allowing someone with little or no income a chance to eventually become an owner. I guess I should have been using the term condo rather than apartment, as they will construct buildings with sales in mind rather than rent.

There were only about twenty of us in camp to hear them explain their project ideas. Other than a couple of "old timers' who are threatened by any real change the mood was electric with the possibility of having a place to call their own.

It became obvious that most in attendance didn't have a clue about financing etc. The questions were pretty good with most being about how soon it would happen. Almost like kids wanting the ice cream before they choke down the liver and onions.

When the visitors left I found myself explaining how mortgages work to about a dozen campers. Makes you wonder what happened to the education system here.

Other than Franz, who has been homeless professionally for years, everyone was positive about the possibility to get an opportunity to move on and up. Franz, the jackass, had a lot of cynical ranting to do about how everyone was out to take advantage of the poor and that these do gooders were looking for a way to make money and didn't care about us a wit. Someone told him to do something remarkable to himself, which got him to push off in a huff. There are moments here that make me proud. If I have the title correct there was a film named "King of Hearts" about the loonies leaving the asylum to get along quite well. I may have that all wrong. Something like that, I think. Doesn't really matter.

# 39

I hope I thanked you for the coffee and English muffin.

I enjoyed hanging out with you kicking around topics other than the obvious. I've definitely missed a lot climbing my inner mountains.

I've thought a lot about what you said about increasing my help to my fellow campers. Most of me knows I have a reserve that can be drawn on to help some of them make a difference in their lives. I feel like a hypocrite at times as I've been swimming in the same sea for such a long time. That there are so many new people here who don't know my history I guess I could step up a bit and see what's to be seen. I don't really care what the old timers think as not much is going to change them no matter what happens.

Funny, Father Jim said pretty much the same to me. Are you guys talking to each other?!

In another life I was all about strategy. Plotting and planning as many steps ahead as I could bring to bear. I remember her telling me that part of me was so calculating and cold that when she noticed it she felt far far away from me. I wonder if she has the interest to look down on how I've handled the gifts I had at one time. God, I am so ashamed of what I've done to bring that look to your face. It's hard to breathe.

Days later.

I've gone through a hard patch the last few days. I feel as if I have something hanging on that I can't quite shake. Tentacles into my mind like the claws that dug into Jesus in the Last Temptation…

More days.

I think I see some light in this fog. I hung out with Father Jim for a day talking about guilt, shame and constantly beating oneself up over all the missteps. Worthless use of limited energy. Enough!

Myrtle. Doesn't that name bring images of cigarettes dangling from over saturated lipsticked lips. Nicotine covered walls in a broken down café. Gazing waitress squinting to avoid the vertical smoke trail serpentining from her mouth into her eyes as she takes your order.

Forget all that, as our Myrtle isn't like that at all. She's a seventy something pound bent over lady waving her gnarled walking stick at anyone who dares get in her way. One of our brighter campers called her a crone one day. He was the recipient of a blur of swordsmanship leaving a huge welt on his forehead. He deserved more.

She's been a bit of a mystery so I decided when given the opportunity I'd shoot the breeze with her.

Ah, the mistakes we make giving into our preconceptions about people.

Myrtle isn't her real name. She told me she choose that after reading about a woman who she respected for her contributions to dance in
a theater in Milwaukee.

She's actually in her early eighties. Can you conceive of living in a
shelter at that age?

I spent a couple of hours talking with her, as she's so interesting.
Why in the world did I pass by her so many times?

She survived the siege on Leningrad. Immigrated to Israel when
the Soviets loosened up in the seventies. Met and married a fellow
Russian, raised two boys who were killed in the West Bank intifada.
Divorced, remarried, widowed and moved to the United States with
who she thought was going to become her husband. In a few months
he left her after investing everything she brought from Israel on a
cockamamie scheme involving exporting soybean oil. She doesn't
know the details and long ago lost interest in any equity regarding her
losses.

She had no one here or back in Israel so did what she had to do to
get a roof over her head. Exactly what that was I am unsure of...

She worked as a domestic cook for a number of families trying to
save whatever she could driven by the hope of perhaps returning to the
new Russia.

One day on her way to work a car hit her as she stepped of the bus.
She sustained back injuries requiring surgery and a long visit in a rehab hospital. Her employer helped out quite a bit though he had no
responsibility to do anything more than what was driven by his generosity. When the expenses became too much he visited her telling her

he just couldn't do any more for her at the time. He told her he would hire her back if she found herself able to work.

When she got out of the hospital she was visited by immigration at the boarding house she moved into with the few pennies to her name. Their visit so frightened her that she called on her previous employer asking for his help. He had hired a replacement but gave her five hundred dollars with the recommendation that she leave Milwaukee as soon as possible.

She moved to Salt Lake City getting café jobs as a short order cook. She knew she could never save enough to return to St. Petersburg. Her back was killing her. She knew she had to do something other than standing over burning hash to make a living. Making survival is more accurate.

I'm a little confused on all the moves after Salt Lake. She came to Seattle about nine months ago with $1,400.00 in her pocket and the plan to teach Russian and Yiddish at a language school in the YMCA. She had gotten a commitment for at least twenty hours a week teaching, which was enough to give her hope. She knew there were a lot of Russian immigrants in Seattle and hoped for the best for the future. When she first got here she was staying at the YWCA a few blocks from where she was to teach. On the second night she was mugged between the two Y's as she walked to work. She was knocked down inflaming her back problems. The aid car took her to Harborview where she was put in traction for ten days. Being the beginning of the term she was replaced at the language school.

When she got out she was broke and desperately afraid that immigration would arrest her. At times she said maybe that would be her way back to Russia though she was too afraid to do anything but try to hide.

So, here she is living in a tent in a major American city selling the world its collective dream of independence and wealth.

I'm way more cynical than she is as she is approaching the Russian immigrant community about moving into a home - apartment house that will be owned by the community for the benefit of their community. It all sounds pretty nice and she is positive about the future. She doesn't seem angry about the twists and turns in her life. I felt good talking to her. I think she enjoyed it as well.

# 40

Brooks Brothers!!! Are you kidding me? A gift certificate to Brooks Brothers!!!! You have completely lost your mind. Lets talk about this when we cross trails.

I visited the main library to find out you can look up people using local phone directories on line. Was an interesting experience to look up few people I knew from the old days in New Jersey.

I came dam close to pulling up old newspaper stories form the UK. Can't believe I almost did that-

She would be looking back at me from the front page of the newspaper wondering why I hadn't taking more care of her security. We were warned. I ignored it.

More young people drifting in here lately.

I didn't notice any copies of Brautigan sticking out of any pockets.

I joined a number of them as they shared coffee and sweets endlessly supplied by volunteers and Starbucks.

(sorry for the Scotch tape here)

Anyway, seems they are on an adventure traveling together living off the land and grid. I had to laugh at their enthusiasm for the road and seeing the "real" America. It's fairly obvious none of them have to live in these conditions but have chosen this as a way to save money and have a place to leave their swag.

They are a little too cynical about the system having a lot to say about the inequities they see surrounding them and their future. When I asked what they were going to do about it the tables got turned on my lifestyle and me. One of the kids was pretty aggressive on me living off the land and generosity of others without contributing to any changes (Since you said you might distribute these ramblings I wont spell out what I wanted to call the little_____).

Well, he was right of course.

Vestis virum reddit! Ok, Brooks Brothers, for God's sake…want to go with me? Maybe they have a Donegal tweed jacket with elbow pads I could get meself.….

41

Sorry, been a while since I last gave you anything to ponder. You are pondering, aren't you?

Before I tell you a tale or two I want to thank you for your time and generosity during our adventure at Brooks Brothers. It was a fun time. Honestly, I can't remember laughing so much or feeling so good about being alive. I wish I could think of a way to repay you.

Funny, my new jacket has put a new color on everything. I feel slightly more confident and less morose. I know this sadness will never leave me and that I need to learn how to love it and incorporate it into my view of the world. I never knew how much I could love someone or how deep I could feel her loss. It was beyond my worst nightmare when she was killed. I need to develop my skills of holding the good from her and not the loss… Father Jim has been an incredible help. You've been a great help just by showing up and guarding your judging. Maybe you should write me telling me what you really think. Never mind! I think I know.

The fire brigade was here checking that no one is unintentionally doing anything that could cause us to flee in a firestorm. Other than a couple of power strips that were bundled they didn't find anything too dangerous. I could tell they wanted to help and not find a bunch of violations. You'd think the cord hanging from the stores power box to our guard shack would have raised some eyebrows. It did but they pretended it was normal. One fire fighter wrapped the cord with tape and secured it to the power box in a better fashion than we had done... Nice to see they were over looking the obvious.

They gave us a number of SFD tee shirts and well-worn jackets. Nice guys.

Bunch of kids dropped by with some cake. They had some event at school, which involved lots of cake and soda. Its fun to see how much they enjoy giving us goodies. They are too young to have developed the questions and shyness that a lot of older kids show when they visit. I think I'd like to share with kids what this is all about.

I have found the doorway out.

If what I've seen the last few years is in any way accurate. I say that as I have doubts about some of my recent memories. Occasionally, I look back and forward with the same bit of awe to the changeling truth. Some thoughts are in diamond and some are smoke. To express an opinion based on any fact makes the second voice inside ridicule the speaking voice. Did I actually say that?

We were invited to a service at the Baptist church. I went to get out of the pouring rain. I don't get it, obviously. Somehow the ability to manifest emotion, speak in tongues fainting from the rapture is way too alien to my experiences. I am so use to the controlled posturing in the high Anglican Church where the only emotion is that hidden one when you put way too much in the collection plate.

Hard to believe I've completely missed on some of what is going on around here. I told you there are twelve step meetings, didn't I? Maybe so much faded to background noise that I can't remember what I've focused on with some of these epistles. Maybe I should call them gospels. Maybe that is too sacrileges! If Jesus didn't have a sense of humor we're all doomed.

Can't seem to focus on my point.

A guy named Mark brought seven speakers to camp to share their stories of drug addiction. Only one of them was over thirty. It was quite the interaction as after each told their tale of woe and climbing back out of the ditch questions were fielded.

A few of your college volunteers were here. They joined in, with one asking why we in this country have so much addiction. In a land so full of grace why is it we want to be so disconnected? Heck of a question.

I went down that road, as I no longer wanted the ability to think. Thinking was too encapsulating. My mind was strangling me without letup. Unconsciousness brought escape for a few precious hours. I didn't realize I was magnifying the problem by tearing my body and mind to shreds. I don't remember which hospitalization brought that thought forward. I've been pretty good since. Well, kinda. A puff here or there.

Listening to all of the guests and residents speak I got the impression that each person has buried deep within fear of being who they are without all the masks. Fear. A friendly bedmate.

All the stuff we have in this society brings the desire and need for more tossing us into a dilemma we aren't rigged to solve.

The majority of girls and women spoke about some kind of abuse as a kid. No one clarified it but it was obvious that the first messages these women got were ones, which underscored their lack of worth.

A couple of our campers spoke about being victims of addiction. They spoke about being unable to do anything because they were held prisoner by the drug. They didn't say it exactly that way but you get the point.

They spoke of helplessness to stop smoking, shooting or drinking as if an alien creature processed them. Knowing a number of smack addicts I can testify to them living only for the drug. Any moral conscious decision-making takes a back seat to the need for the drug. They know its wrong but they'll strip your house or knock you on the head for one more baggy. It's the tweekers you've got to really look out for as their ability to even think about the right or wrong of their action has long ago been suppressed by the insanity of all the poison they are pumping in their bodies.

I don't think I'm doing a great job sharing the conversations as I kept getting left behind as I thought about myself, previous choices and the blessing I have to make changes. Many of them will continue down until the bottom stops or kills them.

No one can really make anyone do anything.

After lively conversation for almost two hours Mark told the campers about three "half way" houses that were recently funded in town. Apartments were going to be available at a reduced rate to people in certifiable programs dealing with whatever addiction was keeping them from moving forward. I could have measured the optimism on a couple of campers faces when they heard about a chance to move with a support system in place (Ok, you've got to return my notes as I feel like I've spoken about this before???).

Mark told them how to get a hold of him and what he was willing to do to support anyone here that really wanted to pursue getting straight on the path of righteousness. I added that last part. He didn't say anything dogmatic at all.

Hope, given a chance can turn even the un-gangliest of rivers.

# 42

Last night, about six o'clock, we got a visit from four MPs accompanied by a Seattle cop. They were looking for deserters. Can't believe it! Deserters!

Not since Nam have I seen any military police sweeping for those gone AWOL, or, the few that have gone totally over the wall

We've had an increase in younger people but I didn't give it much thought to where they might be coming from - things are hard enough without anyone here asking questions they don't need the answers to.

The soldiers didn't find anyone. One be-medaled gunny sergeant reminded us of potential incarceration if we in any way enabled any soldiers on the lamb. Good way to enlist our help! There isn't a snowballs chance in hell that most here would ever say anything about anyone…well, there are a couple of flag wavers who might grass on a deserter. Amazing how some people feel they have the answer for so many others.

Though not the same this reminds me of a preacher who dropped by some months ago to bore us to death with his secret of God's love. Blah blah blah he rattled on telling us how Hell was going to gobble us up in terror if we didn't straighten up and fly right. A couple of campers took a few shots across his bow but he fended them off with his ability to quote the bible like a trained chimp. Why is the ability to quote a book translated as intelligence?????

Intellectual superiority! What! Arrogance is what it is…to out gun people who are obviously less able to kick sand is the real sin.

If Father Jim were here he would have listened to what they had to say and then gently tossed in his thoughts. He always offers a disclaimer, which gives recognition as well as the invitation to listen to the marbles rolling around inside your head. Listen to me, the champion of the church. Scheesch! The electric shock treatment must have burned out some well oiled paths….

I'm on a roll. I had a friend who given the opportunity would slip in "Never tell 'em who shot the truck."

Ok, a little background. He was a "gunslinger" flying the AH-1GHuey Cobra, "The meanest mother ever to take to the skies." One of the rules of the road was to always to work in pairs and never overfly the friendlies. Point being you didn't want your brass cascading down on your own giving them the belief you were firing on them. Anyway, with 4x7.62mm machine guns and 38 2.75in rockets you could definitely give Charlie something to think about as he pulled on his pajamas. You flew in a pattern covering each other's arses as you rained down calamity on whoever was silly enough to garner your at-

120

tention. Freedom comes from God's right hand was painted next to the black cat on the side of the choppers.

In those days the Secretary of War, Robert McNamara, passed down through channels the formulae that professed: X amount of rounds fired equaled Y amount of kills. The famous body count began with everyone reporting how many gooks they smoked when tallying a patrols success story. Sheer insanity brought to us by an intellectual superior elitist with no clue to reality. Truth is we cooked a lot of cattle on the way back to base just to dump some ordinance.

There was a new fresh creased Major who actually believed all the nonsense he learned at the Point. He would require all sorts of reports creating a paper nightmare. We were just out there running and gunning covering pick-ups and the poor guys in the paddies. We didn't need this.

My friend would try to massage the Major but nothing could budge him from his belief that we would win by following McNamara over the cliff. Nothing we said had any impact. Things were reaching the boiling point as the Major was putting us in harms way for no reason. We lost six choppers due to over reaching. Nothing seemed to dent the Majors belief system. Mutiny isn't a word tossed around casually but there was a lot of hot talk among the troops. Things were going to get ugly. Fragging was working its way into too many conversations.

Everything got settled one night as we returned to base. My friend unleashed a number of birds to take out a six by truck sitting about twenty yards east of the Majors command tent. Boom. Warning delivered. Of course the Major demanded to know who shot the truck without success. He got the point-keep it up and a couple of clicks left has you singing with the angels.

So, "Never tell 'em who shot the truck" was the cynical response my friend gave to any situation that might require the truth. The war killed his soul in ways that will show in this Iraq debacle. It bled into relationships ultimately bringing him down to a losing battle with grog. Some years ago we tossed his ashes into the Pacific. He was a good guy not buying into what wasn't important- though he couldn't seem to stop himself. I'm sorry there was nothing to do to help him. Maybe now-maybe not.

All that from a visit from the military. Not a good sign. Love it or leave it!! My sweet Lord, its all illusion, relax!

# 43

Easters is just around the corner. Its nice that we are at a great site with supportive neighbors for the Holydays.

The Reverend has been great. He allows us to use the recreation hall as well as use the showers in the parish building. This is sweet living!!!

There are four or so schools in the neighborhood that have been bringing kid after kid here to play with the campers. I've spotted you a few times leading them around camp. I wanted to say hello but got intercepted by the doings of others.

We haven't really talked since our last coffee. I gave you some information on some relatives of Chelsea. Were you able to find anyone? I've spent some time with her lately.

Chelsea has walked down plenty of challenging roads in her young life.

Seems that older men were Chelsea's salvation and damnation. She once said she didn't like the frenzy around guys her own age. I'm guessing she is under or slightly over forty. Hard to tell as her scar keeps drawing my eyes from the rest of her face. I'd say she is beautiful in a rustic weathered kind of way. I can see her leading a bunch of savvy naturalists through the white water of an approaching five river in Wyoming. Maybe the Wind River?

She moves like a gymnast. Muscles ready to deliver on demand.

She has a disconcerting way of looking at you when engaged in conversation. She puts one finger on her chin and leans into you locking her eyes on yours. I've found I can't hold the gaze very long. I've also found that I am attracted to her. I haven't felt that since before when.

I was slightly surprised when she told me she was born in Iceland. Her given name is Vigdis though she wants to keep that between us. She left Kopavogur when she was twelve with her father and uncle. Her mom had died the previous spring in an auto crash. First they went to Greenland and then to Norway. Her father had a minor position in government responsible for developing sister city relationships. As he wanted to develop a relationship in the states they moved to New York after about a year knocking between Norway and Greenland. She didn't say whether or not the mission was successful. She did say that her uncle taught her that trust was fragile. I presume something happened with him only by the tone of her voice. Listening to her with attention allows me to hear the remnants of her Islenska. It's a bit like German, but different. I like listening to her a lot.

Her father had pushed her to take a course at the local community college to prepare for the tests for citizenship. He enrolled her in a freshman U.S. History class and a tutoring class on civics. Apparently he lied about her age when he enrolled her. She entered the school without challenge. The high school she was enrolled in was far enough from the college that she wasn't concerned about her dual registration or acting older than she was... She really liked hanging out at the college. That she looked older than she was gave her acceptance among the students. After about a year of hanging around the school, in her spare time, she hooked up with a teachers aid she had met through her new college friends. After a time a high school parent visiting the college recognized her creating questions about her age etc. She and her boyfriend headed to Colorado where he had an in at a ski resort. He might not have been the sharpest tool in the shed but he was well aware of what would happen if he were hauled in about a relationship with a girl of fourteen.

As soon as he made contact with his friends in Boulder he dumped her.

I asked about her father. The pause was long and chilly. Her only reply was that she wrote him.

Chelsea was able to get a job as a waitress at the lodge sleeping in the inventory closet. One of the chefs offered her a room above his garage until she could get it together to find her way. She told me he really saved her from grim alternatives being offered. She hung in Boulder working and taking college courses through the mail and extension courses at the University of Colorado at Boulder. She challenged the high school leaving exam receiving a certificate of accomplishment.

Her language abilities plus skill on the hill gave her opportunities to advance in the hospitality arena.  She worked her way up to night manager of the lodge as she finished college.  Everything was rolling along pretty well.  She had a long-term relationship with a ski instructor who also had a job with the airline.  They married when she was 29.  She mentioned traveling to South America with a college professor but I'll leave that story for another day.  There is a bit of singsong in her chronology but I don't care about this being an accurate biography.  I'm just passing it on-

She and her husband joined a ski team shooting to qualify for the Olympics.  They were good and very popular in the ski circles.  She knew she was too old but wanted to give it her all.  They planed and positioned well getting them on the long list of competitors.

The day after her thirtieth birthday she was in a qualifying run on the giant slalom.  The weather was lousy with ground fog hugging ice in some of the turns.  Visibility was limited but she kicked out of the gate with full commitment.

Her next memory is waking up in a full body cast in hospital. Her head was in some contraption with four large screws imbedded in her skull.  She lost it going into a turn catching an edge before she went airborne over the fence.  She broke her legs, back and shoulder.  A ski or pole kicked back gauging its way from the corner of her mouth up through her eye into her hairline.  She didn't know she was pregnant. The baby was lost as well as a good part of some internal organs. She had been in a coma for more than a month.

126

The doctors didn't see her walking too well much less ever skiing again. She would not be able to have children.

Her husband was sincere when he told her he just couldn't live with her in such pain and misery. He had qualified and was leaving for the training camp in upstate New York. His love was finite. He wasn't gone more than weeks when she received notice of divorce proceedings. One of her pals told her he had taken up with one of their other friends.

A month became six. Six became a year as she entered physical therapy for grueling work towards walking again.

(I never would have guessed she had an artificial eye. It explains her intensity) I wanted to draw her into a hug but didn't dare. I'm feeling pretty guilty about that impulse.

It was almost two years before she could manage totally on her own. After months in shock over her abandonment she determined to get on with it. That included developing a relationship with one of her doctors. Time went on with him leaving his wife for her. Boulder was too small to allow them any freedom so they moved to Seattle with him taking a position at a hospital working with injured kids. She entered the cocoon of his life and ambitions putting whatever she dreamed about on hold.

She joined a gym determined to getting herself strong enough to hit the local slopes. The drawback was the incredible pain she was in all the time. She kept it to herself. They made new friends, mostly doctors and their wives. Things were going well until he lost his temper over nothing one evening hitting her in the mouth as she came

127

towards him offering a hug of peace. She went down on her back short-circuiting her in pain. He begged forgiveness but it was done.

I'm going to cut to the chase as I'm finding myself drawn into her story wanting to stay connected by going on and on....

She went to the police who suggested a restraining order and vacate order against him. She couldn't do it until he really beat her one night over flirting with a doctor at a party. She said she didn't but it didn't matter anymore. He was gone and wasn't ever going to come back to her emotionally.

She took everything she could turn into cash and moved in here knowing he would never think to look in a shelter for her. The police are working with her, as is a lawyer. They want to move her to Portland until they can work out the next steps. They are aghast at her living here. They believe drugs have played a role in her husband's behavior. She doesn't care, its done. She referred to herself as a non-painting Frida Kahlo. Too bad!

Easter eggs decorated by second graders. The kids made a lot of cards for us to buck up our situation with their best wishes. Such purity coming from these little souls. As with other notes you can see many hanging from tent poles inside many campers tents. Such a little thing can mean so much. You know this, as I know you organized it. Thanks.

We've been invited to the church for Good Friday and Easter Sunday services. I'm going to go to Father Jim's and attend his service. Me in church, who would believe it?

At our last camp meeting it was brought up that we aren't racially balanced. Can you believe it? A city official comes here with his entourage to tell us to integrate. I have not heard many racial comments or any discussion about keeping this place lily white. Its true the majority of campers are white men followed by a minority of white women. We have had a few dozen black men. I can't remember a black woman, Asian or Latino ever camping with us. Do you think they have stronger community ties than the average white man? Being an expert on being homeless I sure don't have much expertise on the subject.

Are we supposed to go out and recruit for racial balance in our shelter?

Did you ever see the film Thunderheart? The old medicine man tells the Val Kilmer character to be like Mr. Magoo and go up the mountain and get some focus. I laughed out loud at that comment as it wormed home.

Really. Please, city officials, it's about education, housing, health support and a chance to take a swing in the big show.

# 45

Chelsea has left. I'll guess she went to Oregon. She didn't want to be specific though she gave me her lawyer's card along with a hug full of hope and promise. I spent quite a bit of time with her the last couple of weeks. Nothing you need to know. I hope she is able to work her way out of this mess she finds herself in at the moment. Why would anyone try to hurt her? Dam.

I realized I am an "old timer" here. Not a good thing to be. I am not going to let this become my future. I hardly know anyone here anymore. I guess that's a good thing. I wonder how many people have come and gone? No one here keeps any records.

Some high school kids were here Saturday. One of the kids said something about talking with me a year ago. I don't think I was in my talking phase then but it hurt that I have become a fixture. What am I teaching these kids hanging out here?

Had a drug overdose here the other night. Good thing there are enough people here that recognize what's going on with drugs as they helped the guy hang in until the aid car got here. Seattle has got to be the best for emergency calls. They seem to arrive within minutes. Guy was back the next day.

If he'd done that on the streets he would be dead.

My only drugs are a couple of new socially accepted head drugs. I'm not nuts, just blessed. Right!

Hey it may not be fun but its always interesting. Someone famous said that-

As I write this - wrote this, a scream went up which explains the ink line shooting off the page. By the time I jammed this in my pocket and ran up to the front a couple of campers had descended on the tent where the screaming was coming from. A girl I haven't seen before was ushered out and taken into the big mash tent. Seems she was minutes from childbirth. I heard sirens but no aid car appeared. More sirens without an appearance of help. As I was beginning to worry I heard a child cry in the tent. That was easy.

All of us in camp gathered to take a peek at the little tyke. He was wrapped up in one of the SFD tee shirts. The mom radiated. A couple of the women were hovering around her mopping her brow and giving encouraging words. The new mom laughingly said she might name him Mash after the birthplace. I hope she is kidding. It would be a cool nickname but a lousy first name.

The fire department arrived. The EMTs were very complimentary to the help she received telling everyone that they, the firefighters, should have the power to deputize campers like the cops do in certain situations. I was hoping they would be complimentary and they were- helps a lot to kick up some egos that desperately need the boost. One

132

of the fireman said he'd be happy to come and do some advanced first aid training at camp. Sounds like a great idea.

I have no information on the girl who gave birth. I hope she finds a way out of here through the miracle of her son. Not too much to hope for, for a kid born on Holy Thursday.

# 46

Father Jim picked me up early Friday to share breakfast and help out a bit at the church before the Good Friday doings. I feel a little out of place with this, I'm not real sure what I really believe about the whole story. On one level its preposterous. I mean, does any of it make any sense? A glimpse down history seems to show the total absence of any caring God. Don't you think God would be pissed enough of what we've done with the gift of life to reach down and crack a few heads publically.

When I begged all I heard was silence.

I back off with the good Father. He reminds me that I have seen the good and it is in us to realize the truth. Jesuits have a way of leaving me behind with their well-turned arguments. I just can't seem to lean totally into the wind trusting someone else to steer the car. Like I've been so good at it the last few years! Maybe I need to get further out of my own way and let it flow a little more around me. So, if its true that's great-if its not I guess that's as great if it brings some peace.

Thinking about it I realize how many of the people I have dealt with in shelters seem to be the most trusting and hopeful. Is it desperation? Is it recognition and realization given to the most helpless?

Am I fighting the very truth that has been laid on the stoop for me to pick up and run with? Why am I in this endless wresting match? It should be easier!

After I wrote this I went to the library on Saturday to read about the Carmelite St. John of the Cross-, who might have cornered the phrase, "Dark night of the soul." Seems there have been a load of well-known religious people who went through long periods of struggle to the "truths" supporting religion. I read that Mother Teresa may have set the record on her time in the dark. I cant remember his name but some priest who knew her said she found peace with everything before her death. I definitely don't get it!

Happy Easter! Sorry I missed you before your departure to Guate-mala. I think its great your daughter and grandson are going along with you. Not sure I would want to face the kids you are going to see around the dump in Guatemala City. Kids pecking out a living on gar-bage. Maybe the riddle above is solved by the realization some see to the ways to right the wrongs. Is that what all these sages have been trying to show us? Life is what it is but we have a choice on how to dance with it.....

Maybe I'll have all the answers by the time you get back.

# Postscript

When I returned from Guatemala I was so busy with all sorts of things that I didn't get around to visiting the shelter before I headed to Mississippi to join Seattle University students with Katrina relief work. All together I hadn't seen Atreus for almost three months. When I eventually went by camp I was told he had left. He had left the last few notes for me. I consider it a minor miracle that I got them.

I wasn't too concerned with him being gone, as he had left town a number of times before returning eventually. I recall only hoping he was all right.

Months passed before I heard from him. I received a letter from him sent to our company post box.

Funny. I waited a couple of days before I opened it. Not sure why I held off.

Here is a bit of his letter.

*...Here I sit at a Starbucks pounding away on an Apple laptop. Bet you wish I had typed some of my scribbling to you!*

*As I sit here wondering what to write I noticed what the quote is on my latte cup. "Love Wins"*

*Kind of like getting the just right fortune cookie or astrological forecast when you need it.*

*Thanks Starbucks for all of what you do…*

*Shortly after meeting Father Jim, particularly after my dinner with him, I asked him for help on reaching out to what family I have left. I wanted to ask you but I now realize I didn't because I would have been so embarrassed if you went into hyper drive for me and I fell on my face. I think priests have an easier time dealing with people falling on their good intentions. I hope you don't feel bad that I never mentioned anything. If this hurts you I am sorry.*

*My family consists of a brother in law and his family. After Rebecca and my collapse I got as far away from them and all reminders both consciously and unconsciously. I could back space but I'm going to leave that as is.*

*Father Jim spent a lot of time with me giving me the balance for him to take the next steps. When he first spoke to my brother in law he was told that they knew I was in Seattle. All this time I thought anyone who knew me probably figured I was long dead. When I was busted for my shopping mall caper the cops ran my prints to determine if they had found Jimmy Hoffa etc. Well, my family had a private investigator on retainer who scanned my name, prints, description etc on a fairly regular basis. He informed the family of the warrant search by the police. They decided to do nothing. Too much time and damage had gone under the bridge for them to reach out to what I had become.*

138

*They didn't know what to do so they did what I would probably have done. Nothing. They knew about my stay in California before my Washington days.*

*When Father got them they were not exactly overjoyed though they said they were happy that I was all right and taking some care of myself.*

*Time and Father Jim's phone calls smoothed the waters. It was some months before I spoke to any of them. That was a rough call. I couldn't hold it together when I spoke about Rebecca. There were enough tears to go around. The kids told me how much they had missed me, which made it easier.*

*Things moved faster than I would have thought. I agreed to certain things I would do and they agreed to let me stay in a guesthouse until we all figured out the next steps. The good news for me is that no one ever considered me dead and buried so my interests in the family business continued to accrue value. Obviously, I have no position there but I have the means to stay afloat fairly comfortably. Seems that a lot of things were working in my behalf while I was floundering around myself. It is what it should have been so no need to waste a lot of time on should of-could of.*

*Vigdis joined me a couple of weeks ago. It will take enormous effort on both of our parts to hold what we think we may have captured.*

*Enclosed is a cashier check, which should cover pizzas for the camp. We've talked about doing something on a regular basis to help you and the campers out. There are things to sort out here so I'm not in a position to make any promises - yet.*

*We're thinking about moving to Boston or New York. Not in the city but close. Father Jim has some fellow Jesuits who may need some help with their work with kids on the streets. We'll see.*

*Thanks for everything. I miss Sage and - you.*

National Alliance to End Homelessness
Statistics as of October 2007


Over the course of a year, between 2.5 and 3.5 million Americans will live either on the streets or in an emergency shelter.

Over 5 million low-income households have serious housing problems due to high housing costs, substandard housing conditions, or both.

Within 2-4 years of exiting foster care, 25 per- cent of foster children experience homelessness.

About 600,000 families and 1.35 million children experience homelessness in the US each year, and about 50 percent of the total homeless population is a part of a family.

It is estimated that between 23 and 40 percent of homeless adults are veterans.

The rate of HIV infection in the homeless population is three times higher than that of the general population.

Homeless children go hungry twice as often as other children.

In rural areas, families, single mothers, and children make up the largest group of people who are homeless.

# The Committee to End Homelessness in King County, Seattle, Washington

Although the program-by-program results for 2007 will not be compiled for several months, it is useful to reflect at this time on whether we are showing success in the key areas we are addressing.

Are we preventing people from becoming homeless?

In 2006 we prevented over 3,000 people from becoming homeless and expect similar results for 2007. We are in the process of expanding those efforts through an application for a major state grant in the range for $3 million for prevention services.

Equally important, for the first time we are coordinating our prevention efforts, as King County and the City of Seattle combined $2.55 million in funding from the Veterans and Human Service Levy, CDBG, Seattle Housing Levy and Seattle General Fund to create a coordinated housing stability system, with consistent qualifications and evaluations. We expect a major grant this spring from state HGAP funding for our prevention efforts.

Are we moving people rapidly from homelessness to housing?

143

Even as we seek to increase our pace of production, our programs are showing incredible success.

Through the Bill and Melinda Gates Foundation's Sound Families programs, 1,487 families (4,455 individuals) were served and as of June 2007:

* 64% of the families had been homeless before, some four or more times.

* Among those successfully completing the transitional stay within their program, 89% were able to secure permanent housing after exit.

* Full time employment tripled from entry to exit.

* After analyzing the data from Sound Families on families who were not successful, we have created new programs to address those families.

DESC's 1811 Eastlake took in 75 of the very hardest to serve, people who on average had been homeless 31 of the 36 months prior to moving in.

* Only 16 (21%) of those returned to the street

* Overall the project showed cost avoidance from reduced medical, jail and other emergency services, of over $2.5 million a year.

• The Metropolitan Improvement District reported a 48% decrease in alcohol related incidents and a 21% decrease in calls for the County sobering van.

Plymouth Housing's "Begin at Home" program also addressed high utilizers. This involved 20 people with at least $10,000 annual cost at Harborview or at least 60 visits to the Sobering Center.

* Only one person was evicted in a year

* The program reported acute care service cost avoidance of approximately $1.5 million in the first year.

Although these are just examples of the uses to which we have put the 1,489 units we have brought on line or the 1,291 units we have in the pipeline, similar successes are shown in the other programs. We expect that when the end-of-year data is in we will have helped well over 2,500 people move from homelessness to permanent housing in 2007.

Are we increasing the efficiency of the existing system?

Our work coordinating funding has been recognized as a best practice by the National Alliance to End Homelessness and Corporation for Supportive Housing. In 2007, funders coordinated $31 million through this process, with more than $15 million for homeless housing and services.

Similarly, our Landlord Liaison project combines funding from King County, City of Seattle and United Way to create a coordinated, multi-element system for accessing the private landlord market. In service delivery we are bringing together previously fragmented portions of our system as in the unified prevention work described above.

Are we building public and political will to end homelessness?

We have achieved endorsement by municipalities covering over 84% of the population of King County and have four additional endorsements pending. We have a speakers bureau talking to civic and business groups. Our video has been featured on a number of web sites. We have had symposia and conferences including the Community Resource Exchange and Faith Community symposium in November.

Through direct contacts and press releases we have been able to place or inspire a steady stream of newspaper articles and editorials in both the major dailies and in the regional papers. The Eastside Human Services Forum has adopted a sub-regional plan to end homelessness on the Eastside, and a similar plan is being developed for South County. One of the great examples of the level of public will that exists is United Way's undertaking to raise $25 million above and beyond all of its other fundraising to address chronic homelessness.

We created a joint advocacy agenda with a broad coalition of affordable housing advocates and homeless housing and services advocates across the state. This unified voice resulted in significant successes in the 2007 session and looks to achieve similar successes in the short 2008 session (of the $232 million in the Governor's supplemental budget request, $56 million is housing or homeless services).

Are we tracking success and measuring results?

The HMIS system delivered its first set of data analysis last fall, and a major upgrade is expected shortly. In the meantime we have outcome measurements in all of our programs, and are tracking advances in housing status, housing stability, employment and the like. As noted above, data summaries for 2007 should be available in the early spring of 2008.